THE
MUDDLEMOOR
MYSTERIES

PERIL

AT THE

BAKE

OFF

D0583141

THE MUDDLEMOOR MYSTERIES

PERIL
AT THE
BAKE OFF

by **Ruth Quayle**
illustrated by
Marta Kissi

Andersen Press

First published in 2021 by
Andersen Press Limited
20 Vauxhall Bridge Road
London SW1V 2SA
www.andersenpress.co.uk

2 4 6 8 10 9 7 5 3 1

British Library Cataloguing in Publication Data available.

ISBN 978 1 83913 009 0

Printed and bound in Great Britain by Clays Ltd, Elcograf S.p.A.

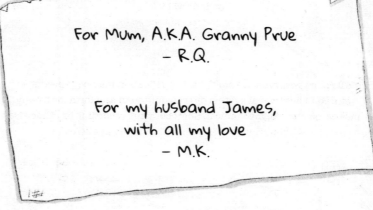

For Mum, A.K.A. Granny Prue
– R.Q.

For my husband James,
with all my love
– M.K.

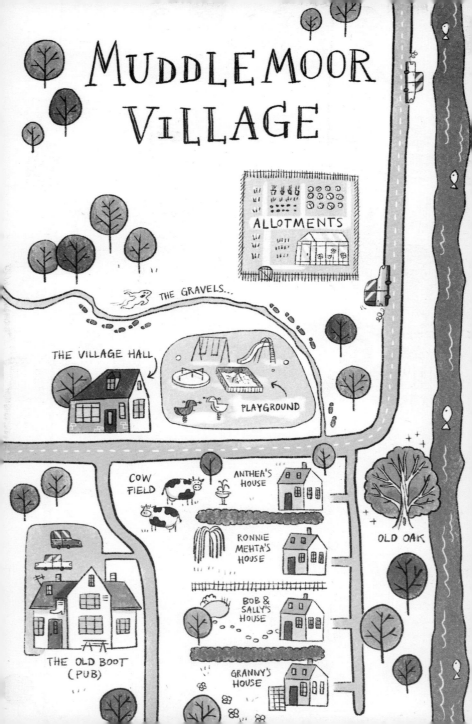

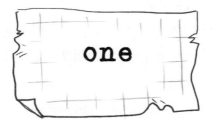

one

When people call me 'Joey' I say, 'Who's Joey?' If people shout 'Joseph', I have trouble hearing them. I am not called Joey or Joseph or Jojo or J. I am **Joe Robinson** and that is that.

My family is on the small side, just me and Mum most of the time. Sometimes my sister Bella comes home from university, but she doesn't count because she's too old to play fun games. Mum says it's a good job there aren't more Joe Robinsons in our family because she has trouble keeping

JOE ROBINSON

up with just one version. But I don't think I'd mind more of me because I am quite friendly and also I'm a chatterbox. Mum says I could talk the hind legs off a donkey, but I would NEVER do that because I LOVE donkeys and wouldn't want them to lose their back legs. I might be a vet one day – or maybe a hamster trainer.

Normally in the school holidays when Mum has to work, I go to the holiday club at our local leisure centre, but this summer Mum made a big announcement. She said there had been a change of plan and I was going to stay with my **granny** in Muddlemoor instead.

GRANNY

(Muddlemoor is the name of Granny's village. It is in the countryside, a long way from where I live in London).

When Mum told me this I looked her straight in the eyes to

check she wasn't joking because it is really **good** at Granny's house. It is better than the holiday club. But even though I was happy I also felt slightly nervous because one thing I have never done is stay at Granny's on my own. Mainly Mum comes with me and sometimes Bella, too.

'Will me and Granny have enough to talk about?' I asked.

Mum laughed and said, 'Running out of conversation is not exactly a problem for you, Joe Robinson.'

And I nodded because that was quite a good point of Mum's. But then Mum said something that stopped me worrying about running out of conversation with Granny. She told me that my cousins Tom and Pip Berryman were also going to be staying in Muddlemoor **WITHOUT THEIR PARENTS.**

At this point I got a bit hyper because me and my cousins get on like a house on fire. The handy thing about cousins is that they're not as cross as brothers and sisters but they know you better than your friends do.

Like for instance, at my school in London, people think I make things up and they sometimes say I'm REALLY SILLY, but Tom and Pip don't think being silly is a bad thing. One day I would like to bring Tom and Pip into my school and show them to the Year Sixes. Even Dylan Moynihan would be impressed with my cousins.

Tom is one year and four months older than me and he knows a lot about dinosaurs and the solar system and why the world exists. Tom always knows about stuff before everybody else finds out. In Wales, where he lives, Tom has a girlfriend called Carys Jones who he loves even though he hasn't spoken to her yet. Tom is really fast at running and good at catching balls and he is also a bookworm. For example, he doesn't just read a few pages of his book at bedtime like I do, he reads in broad daylight whenever he fancies. He even reads when the telly is on – that's how much Tom loves books.

Mum says Tom is so sharp he'll cut himself. But once,

when Tom did actually cut himself on a tin of tuna, he cried like crazy even though it wasn't even that bad and didn't need stitches, just a waterproof plaster.

Pip is eight months younger than me, but she is strong – especially when it comes to doing cartwheels and headstands. Pip doesn't say much, but she isn't shy, she's just keener on thinking. Pip NEVER cries. If Pip came to my school I would ask her to do backflips at breaktime.

The grown-ups in our family call me, Tom and Pip the Terrible Trio and they wink at each other as if we can't see them (but we can because our eyes are always peeled and we don't like to miss a trick). Mum says that when me, Tom and Pip

TOM AND PIP

are together we go round looking for trouble, but she has got her facts wrong because, for a start, when we go to stay with them in Wales or we all go to Granny's house, Mum is mainly chatting to the grown-ups and not even paying attention to what we're up to.

Tom says the grown-ups in our family are lucky that we are so good at looking after ourselves because while they are chatting and drinking wine we are usually in grave danger. The swear-on-my-life truth is that we don't go round looking for trouble. Trouble comes looking for us. It just arrives.

It turned out this summer that most of the time Granny was too busy baking cakes and listening to the radio to worry about what we were up to. She mainly thought we were upstairs playing Lego. Sometimes she didn't even ask questions when we came through the back door covered in mud with suspicious cuts and bruises all over our arms and legs. She'd just say, 'Oh isn't it lovely to see proper grubby knees,' and run us a bath.

I am not mad about baths, but I was pleased that Granny didn't ask too many questions. I was also happy that she didn't take us to museums like some grannies do.

But then Granny DID start asking questions for a change and that's because me, Tom and Pip did something REALLY BAD.

Tom said it was the worst thing he had ever done. Mum said it was even more serious than when I flooded the school toilets. Granny told us that if we did anything like that again, she **would** start taking us to museums.

THAT'S how cross she was. But the thing is, we didn't mean to be bad. We were ONLY trying to help.

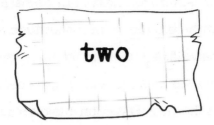

two

I t took me and Mum nearly three hours to drive to Muddlemoor because there was a lot of holiday traffic. It was nearly three o'clock in the afternoon when we parked outside Granny's house. Tom and Pip were already there. Pip rushed out to our car straight away to meet us. She didn't say much but she smiled and helped carry my bag upstairs to the bedroom I was sharing with her and Tom.

After a few minutes, Tom wandered into the kitchen, all cheerful, carrying a letter in his hand. 'Sorry,' he said, 'I was catching up on my correspondence.' Mum raised her eyebrows and gave Granny a look, but I don't think Tom noticed the look because he was too busy stealing biscuits from the tin in the larder and putting them in his rucksack. After Mum left to drive back to London, Tom shared the biscuits with me and Pip and showed us round the village.

Tom knew Muddlemoor off by heart because, unlike me and Pip, he had stayed on his own with Granny once before. He led us down Little Draycott (which is the name of Granny's lane) and turned left on to Stonely Road. We walked past the village hall and a dilapidated tennis court, and we looked through the window of the village shop (which was run by a very tall woman with spiky hair called Mrs Rooney). At the end of Cuddingmill Road we stopped in front of a big red-brick house with chickens in the front garden.

'Most expensive house in the village,' said Tom. 'The owners only come here during the holidays and occasional weekends. They live abroad most of the time.'

'How do you know?' I asked.

'Sophie Pearce told me. She looks after their chickens. Sophie Pearce looks after everybody's chickens. She goes to secondary school and has a gold mobile phone.'

Tom went a bit red. He said, 'Sophie Pearce is an interesting person,' and then he told me and Pip to be quiet and stop winding him up, even though we weren't saying anything.

We walked on in silence and after a few seconds, Tom said, 'That's where Sophie Pearce lives,' and walked us down a no-through road called Church Lane.

Like most roads in Muddlemoor, Church Lane seemed very quiet and safe compared to the crowded London streets that I was used to, but when I pointed this out Tom said, 'Don't judge a book by its cover.'

I was about to ask Tom to explain what he meant, but he showed us a modern house with a tidy front garden and said, 'That's Sophie Pearce's house.'

At that moment the front door of the house opened and a girl with black curly hair and hoop earrings came out.

'Oh,' she said, tapping into a gold mobile phone. 'Hi.'

Tom went bright red and didn't say anything.

'Everything OK?'

Tom just stared.

'Well,' said Sophie Pearce, looking bored. 'Bye then.'

As soon as Sophie Pearce turned the corner towards the bus stop, Tom said, 'Split!' and we raced after him all the way back to the shop.

'Was that Sophie Pearce?' asked Pip.

'Yes.'

'I thought you knew her.'

'I do.'

'Then why didn't you speak to her?'

Tom told Pip to stop being so nosy or else, and then he went into the shop to buy wine gums because Tom never gets tired of wine gums. He once ate sixty-two in one go.

We had nearly enough money between us for a small pack of wine gums and three lollies. We asked Mrs Rooney if we could come back later with the one penny we owed her, but she said, 'I'm not a bank. I don't do credit,' and carried on watching the telly on the wall above the counter.

So we had to swap the wine gums for a packet of

chocolate buttons because chocolate buttons are always the cheapest thing you can buy, even in London.

'They'll rot your teeth,' Mrs Rooney shouted as we left her shop, but I didn't mind because when it comes to teeth I am not much of a worrier.

'This is much more fun than doing multi-skills at the leisure centre,' I said as we walked back to Granny's house.

'More dangerous though,' said Tom. 'That's something I discovered when I stayed here on my own in the Easter holidays. Granny's village is a hotspot for crime.'

I went a bit gulpy. 'Are you sure?'

''Fraid so,' said Tom. 'In the Easter holidays I spotted suspicious activity from morning till night. Missing lipsticks, mail going walkabout – you name it. An innocent pensioner from Tiddlington Road died in her sleep one night – they said it was old age but they would, wouldn't they?'

I nodded but I was not quite sure. Tom pointed to a

narrow, overgrown path on our left.

'See that path?' he said. 'It's called The Gravels. It's a shortcut back to Granny's but my advice is, don't ever go down there if you can help it. It's haunted.'

I looked at the overgrown path and shivered.

'At Granny's you have to concentrate even when you're watching telly,' said Tom. 'And the weird thing is, Granny never seems to notice.'

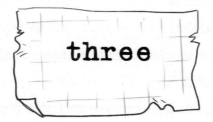

three

For the next few days I did what Tom said. I looked out for suspicious activity in the village. I paid attention, even when I was watching telly. I also had a good look at Granny's nearest neighbours, e.g. Bob and Sally Merry next door and Ronnie Mehta at Number Six, but everyone seemed quite friendly and Muddlemoor was actually REALLY quiet. The only thing that went missing was Granny's recycling bin, but Bob and Sally admitted that they had taken it by mistake and even Tom believed them.

Sometimes we went for walks all around the village (although we NEVER walked through The Gravels, not even when we were in a hurry). Soon me and Pip knew our way around nearly as well as Tom did.

We also got to know some of the other people who lived in Muddlemoor, e.g. Chris Norris who only had one arm and smoked cigarettes AT THE SAME TIME AS RIDING HIS BIKE.

We really liked bumping into the Fletton twins because they'd always throw their shoes out of their buggy and shout, 'Go away!' at strangers.

One person we weren't so keen on was Granny's friend Anthea. Anthea had a loud voice that boomed and she was always asking people to pick up their dog poo. Granny told us that Anthea was much cleverer than most people and that she used to have a very important job inventing robots for the British government.

Even though Anthea was now mainly retired, that didn't stop her asking us tricky questions, such as, what is the capital of Iceland? Or, who is the president of Ukraine? And I'm not good at tricky questions. Tricky questions are harder than French.

Once, Anthea invited us round for biscuits and

Ribena but even though me and my cousins love biscuits and Ribena, and even though Anthea has a massive garden with a really good swing in it, we did not go because of the questions and also because Anthea's house smells of cat litter trays. Anthea is crazy about cats. She has seven.

Another time, Anthea asked us if we wanted to go birdwatching with her, but we made up a good excuse because birdwatching with Anthea sounded too educational and I worried it would take AGES.

Sometimes we saw Sophie Pearce around the village. Once, when we were in the park behind the school, Sophie came and sat on the swings with us. She told us that people in the village paid her four pounds per day to look after their chickens when they were on holiday.

Whenever Sophie Pearce was around, Tom stopped speaking, but I don't think Sophie Pearce noticed because she was always on her phone.

Mainly though, we played football and ate ice lollies. Luckily our granny was calm and collected. Also, she was nicer than our parents. Like for instance, she didn't start nagging if we left dirty clothes on the floor and she never even noticed if we nibbled a KitKat before dinner. When I asked her if I could leave my bedside light on all night, she said, 'I don't see why not,' in a really kind voice.

Granny told us that the best part about being a granny is that she gets to ignore things like homework and table manners and concentrate on the fun stuff. Fun stuff is fine by us. Granny also told us that she is very keen on children being free and independent and not relying on grown-ups to entertain them. She is especially keen on children being free and independent when it's time for her to watch *Cul-de-Sac* on the telly.

Cul-de-Sac is Granny's favourite thing in the universe. It is a programme about a woman called Sheila who is always having arguments with a man called Phil. Phil might be Sheila's husband or he might be her dad but I am not a hundred per cent sure because Granny won't answer questions when *Cul-de-Sac* is on, not even if we whisper. And when *Cul-de-Sac* isn't on, I forget to ask her.

I once asked Granny if she was addicted to *Cul-de-Sac* and she said, 'That's right, my boy, dangerously addicted. Hook, line and sinker.'

And she wasn't even joking.

This made Tom a bit worried because he said when people are addicted to something it is **NOT HEALTHY**. Tom said that his dad, who is my uncle Marcus, used to be addicted to smoking cigarettes and now he has to chew gum for the rest of his life. Tom and Pip's dad is very clever, but Mum says he is also a know-it-all so the clever bit doesn't count as much.

Anyway, **APART** from being addicted to *Cul-de-Sac* our Granny is **MAINLY** calm and collected. But one day, in the middle of the summer holidays, she started acting **QUITE** weird and stressed out, and me and my cousins could not help noticing because it was **REALLY** obvious.

four

I t all started when Mrs Rooney in the village shop showed Granny a poster about the Great Village Bake Off which was happening that Sunday.

'Oh help,' said Granny. 'Is it really that time of year again? I'd forgotten.'

'You need to get practising like everybody else,' said Mrs Rooney. 'I've sold more self-raising flour these past few days than the rest of the year put together. Bob Merry bought three dozen eggs yesterday.'

Granny groaned. 'Come on, you lot,' she said. 'I'm going to need your help.'

On the way home, Granny explained that in Muddlemoor the Great Village Bake Off is bigger than the World Cup Final. Everybody takes it really seriously because they all want to win.

Granny said that in Muddlemoor there are a lot of keen bakers, like for example Bob Merry who used to be a chef, and Anthea who is FIERCELY COMPETITIVE. Even Ronnie Mehta enters the Bake Off and he never cooks if he can help it.

As soon as Granny found out that the Great Village Bake Off was happening on Sunday she forgot about taking us to the adventure playground and made us go to Sainsbury's. She even forgot to cook dinner and we had to have cereal instead.

This is because she was so busy thinking about what she could bake to win this year's Bake Off.

Luckily, on Friday, when she was rummaging around in the attic for the old Monopoly board, Granny found a long-lost recipe for chocolate fudge layer cake that had been invented by HER grandmother.

Granny told us it was an exciting discovery. She said it was better than digging up priceless treasure. Except in my opinion that old recipe didn't look like priceless treasure because the paper was crinkly and the writing was all crossed out and wiggly and **IMPOSSIBLE TO READ.** But this didn't stop Granny being over the moon with happiness.

The next morning, Granny said, 'Don't for goodness sake tell anyone else about this secret recipe.' She popped the scrappy bit of paper on the kitchen island and studied it for the twenty-seventh time. 'Those neighbours of mine would do **ANYTHING** to get their hands on this!'

When Granny said this, Tom kicked me and Pip under the table and gave us a serious look and, instead of running off to play football (which is what we normally do after breakfast), he called an emergency summit in our bedroom.

'I knew something like this would happen,' he said.
'Didn't I warn you this village is a hotspot for crime? Did
you hear what Granny said? Those criminal neighbours
are trying to get their hands on her recipe.'

When it comes to spotting criminal activity Tom is
nearly always one step ahead.

'What shall we do?' I asked.

'There is only one thing we can do,' said Tom. 'We'll

just have to stay inside until Sunday and guard that recipe.'

'Oh right,' I said and I was a bit disappointed about this because it was a really sunny day and we had been planning to go down to the tadpole stream to find Roman coins.

Granny said she needed to bake three sponge cakes because the chocolate fudge layer cake had three layers. She said if we liked we could help her bake Layer Number One.

Pip asked if she could break the eggs and Tom melted the chocolate and I got to pour in the flour. Except it is hard to pour flour neatly when you're also keeping an eye on a secret recipe. That's why things got a bit messy.

Normally Granny is fine about a bit of mess when we're baking, but because the Great Village Bake Off is a serious baking competition, she kept saying, 'Hang on,

HANG ON!' And, 'How many eggs went in there?'

And then she got really stressed and told us to burn off some steam in the garden instead.

And even though she wasn't exactly cross, we also knew that she meant business because when grown-ups tell you to 'Burn off steam' or 'Get some fresh air' what they really mean is, 'Go away'.

In fact, grown-ups are always telling us to burn off steam just when things are getting interesting.

But that morning it was a good thing that Granny told us to burn off some steam because if we hadn't gone outside we would NEVER have found out exactly WHO was trying to get their hands on Granny's secret recipe . . .

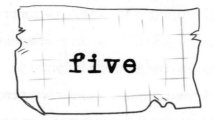

five

At home, I would not climb into other people's gardens. That's because some of our neighbours have big dogs and some have barbed wire on the tops of their walls, and also most of them shout at me.

But in Granny's village there isn't any barbed wire and the dogs are mainly smallish. Plus, Granny's neighbours don't shout at you if you climb into their gardens. They LIKE it.

For instance, Bob and Sally Merry don't ever get grumpy when we sneak through the gap in their hedge and use their garden as a shortcut. Bob used to be a chef and Sally used to be a dentist and even though they're really keen on keeping their garden neat and tidy they let us climb their apple tree.

Once Sally asked us if we wanted to see pictures of their holiday house in Italy, but I explained that we couldn't because looking at other people's holiday house photos is one thing that makes me really fidgety. I was not even joking when I said this but Bob snorted with laughter and said I was a hoot.

On Tuesday nights, Bob and Sally go to Italian lessons in the village hall with a teacher called Mario. Bob and

Sally think Mario knows everything there is to know about Italy, but one time Granny went with them and she said Mario had a Scottish accent and kept having to look up words in a dictionary.

Next to Bob and Sally is Ronnie Mehta. Ronnie Mehta doesn't go in his garden much because he sells houses for a living and is always inside on his phone doing deals. Ronnie Mehta's children don't go in the garden either because they are teenagers.

Ronnie Mehta says we're welcome anytime because it's nice to see his garden being used.

On the other side of Ronnie Mehta's hedge is Anthea's garden, but we don't dare go in there because remember what I said about Anthea not being our most favourite person on the planet.

Tom says whenever he goes near Anthea, something bad seems to happen to him. He is not even joking. At Easter when he was staying at Granny's on his own he climbed the hedge into Anthea's back garden for a challenge and just as his feet landed on Anthea's grass there was a massive clap of thunder and then there was a gigantic bolt of lightning in the sky. And Tom had to climb back over that hedge in a jiffy and he ripped his knee on a sharp piece of cement and he was IN AGONY for the whole night.

When Anthea is around, Pip goes even quieter than usual. And that is saying something because Pip is already the quietest member of our family.

Mum says that Pip is a thinker and thinkers tend to

talk less than most people. When I asked Mum if I am a thinker like Pip, she laughed so much she spilled tea all over the food mixer. 'No, Joe Robinson,' she said, 'you are not a thinker. You do most things in life WITHOUT thinking.' And then she smiled and ruffled my hair and made me some peanut butter on toast.

But even though I'm not one of life's thinkers, I know exactly why Pip goes extra specially quiet when Anthea is around. Because even though Anthea likes cats and birdwatching and all the other things that lots of old people like, there is something CREEPY about her. Which is why, that morning, we stopped when we got to Anthea's hedge and headed inside Ronnie Mehta's weeping willow instead.

Ronnie Mehta's weeping willow tree is a good place for hiding from grown-ups because the branches come right down to the ground. The inside is a bit like a cave but better because it's not creepy or covered in slimy seaweed.

When we were inside the weeping willow we'd

mainly sit on the ground, but if it was wet and muddy we'd take turns to sit on a plastic stool we borrowed from Granny's shed. Except Pip didn't mind skipping her turns because she was keener on doing handstands against the trunk. Muddy hands do not bother my cousin Pip.

Apart from the plastic stool the only other thing inside that willow tree was an old black tin where we kept sweets and private things, like stink bombs and fart powder and some capsules that make you look like you have blood pouring out of your mouth.

That tin was our private property because it came with its own padlock and Pip told me she was going to wear the key to the padlock on a chain around her neck at all times, including when she went back to school, even though she isn't allowed to wear jewellery at her school. (One of the best things about Pip is that she is not scared of breaking rules.)

We sat down next to the tree trunk and Tom got some biscuits out of his rucksack and Pip did a handstand

and I started chatting about polar bears because polar bears are one of my favourite subjects of conversation, but then I had to stop chatting about polar bears because we heard a loud voice.

'Morning, Anthea!'

We peered through the branches and saw Ronnie Mehta leaning on the hedge. He had a phone in one hand and a coffee in the other and he was talking to Anthea. 'I'm surprised you're not inside baking your entry for the Great Village Bake Off on Sunday,' said Ronnie.

Anthea laughed. 'Still trying to decide what to bake. Might have to pull an all-nighter. What about you?'

'Ah,' said Ronnie Mehta, 'that's classified information, Anthea. If I told you, I'd have to kill you.'

Anthea and Ronnie both burst out laughing, but me, Pip and Tom did not laugh because in our opinion murder is not a laughing matter.

'It's Jenny we have to worry about this year,' said a quiet, gentle voice coming from the opposite direction.

We spun round and looked through another curtain of leaves and there was Bob peering over his fence.

At this point we decided to listen REALLY CAREFULLY because Jenny is our granny's real name. And, even though Bob has a quiet, gentle voice,

when it comes to Granny's neighbours Tom says you can never be too sure.

'I've just spoken to her. She's working on some rare, secret recipe she dug out of the attic,' said Bob, 'and from what I gather she's feeling PRRRREEEEEETTTTY confident about her chances.'

Anthea laughed loudly. 'How mysterious! She said the same to me on the phone just now. She wouldn't tell me anything more about it, though.'

Then Bob Merry went back to his weeding.

Ronnie Mehta raised his eyebrows and winked. 'Well, Anthea,' he said, 'you'd better come up with a plan fast, hadn't you.'

Anthea laughed again. 'You know me, Ron,' she said. 'Once a spy, always a spy . . .'

Me, Tom and Pip gasped and STARED at each other.

We were SO SHOCKED.

We were utterly flabbergasted.

Anthea had just admitted in BROAD DAYLIGHT that she was a SPY.

Suddenly everything went middle-of-the-night quiet. Middle-of-the-night quiet is even quieter than school-assessment quiet.

At home when I wake up in the middle of the night feeling hungry, I can't even steal a biscuit without Mum hearing me because at three-thirty in the morning a chair moving GENTLY on the kitchen floor sounds REALLY NOISY.

'Talking of spying' said Anthea, lowering her voice to a whisper, 'I've found a good lookout spot in Jeffrey's meadow. I'm going to hide out there – see if I can lay eyes on our elusive friend.'

I gasped so loudly that Tom had to put his hands over my mouth. Anthea glanced over at the willow tree and we all held our breath.

'Hmmmmm,' said Anthea. 'Anyway, no time like the present. I'm off now as it happens. I'd like to get a sighting before lunch.'

Ronnie Mehta waved.

'Keep me posted, Anthea.'

'Righto!'

Anthea's footsteps got fainter as she walked away from the weeping willow tree.

'Off you go, Pozo,' she said to one of her cats, pushing him back towards the house. 'I can't have you blowing my cover with that bell of yours.'

(Anthea's cats wear collars with bells to warn small animals and birds that they are coming.)

We crept out of our hiding spot and peered over the hedge into Anthea's garden. Anthea walked to the end of her garden, climbed the fence and set off across Jeffrey's meadow (which we call the cow field).

'See,' said Tom, 'she's trying to get a sighting of something and I bet that something is Granny's secret recipe.'

I was not sure if Tom was a hundred per cent correct about this, but then I noticed that Anthea was carrying something around her neck and when I looked more closely I realised that maybe Tom had a point after all because it was a MASSIVE pair of binoculars.

six

'**D**idn't I tell you this village is a hotspot for crime?' said Tom. 'We're going to have to follow Anthea to see what she's up to.'

We made our way to the end of Ronnie Mehta's garden and crouched among the trees and bushes. Anthea strode quickly across the cow field, moving further away from us.

'We'll have to go over the fence,' said Tom.

This made my heart thump really loudly because one thing I did **NOT** want to do was go into the cow field. The one time I went in there to try to rescue our football, I got really badly chased by the cows and was nearly trampled to death.

I tried suggesting to Tom and Pip that we could still keep an eye on Anthea WITHOUT going in the cow field, but Tom said that when you are trying to save your granny from her evil and dangerous neighbour you have to take the occasional risk, e.g. being trampled by cows.

Tom and Pip climbed over the fence and set off across Jeffrey's meadow (A.K.A. the cow field) on their hands and knees, trying to keep up with Anthea's long strides. Even though the cows were a long way off in the distance they kept making sneezing noises and looking over at Tom and Pip. I crossed my fingers and followed them.

Eventually, Anthea reached the woods at the far end of the cow field and stopped walking. She pointed her enormous pair of binoculars at the trees. We ducked down and watched.

'What's she doing?' I asked, wriggling. The grass felt hot and scratchy.

'I'm not sure,' said Tom. 'But one thing is certain: Anthea is obsessed with Granny's recipe and when people are obsessed with something, it can have tragic consequences.'

Tom told us that a boy in his class called Freddie Marriot was so obsessed with chocolate that he once stole a Twix from his teacher's desk and ate it in class. But even though this was a serious crime, Freddie Marriot did not get in big trouble because when he was sent to the headteacher he cried a lot and explained that he was obsessed with chocolate and the headteacher said, 'Never mind, Freddie, we all have our weaknesses,' and when Freddie came back to class he stopped crying and told the teacher he would buy her a new Twix.

But then a few days later at the school Christmas lunch Freddie Marriot pinched so many chocolate coins he was sick down Betsy Brown-Taylor's brand-new reindeer sequin jumper and he had go home and miss the trip to see Dick Whittington at the panto – and that shows how dangerous obsession can be because missing the Christmas panto is A TRAGEDY.

Thinking about Freddie Marriot made ME feel a bit sick so I suggested going back to Granny's to play football because football is one thing that always stops you feeling sick.

But Tom said we couldn't leave Anthea to her own devices. He said we had to find out what she was up to.

There were not many clouds in the sky and I started to get really hot, lying in the middle of the cow field in the midday sun.

'Give her five more minutes,' said Tom, holding his finger to his lips. 'I KNOW she's up to something.'

A few minutes later Anthea set off across the cow field again.

'See!' said Tom and started scrambling along the ground after her.

Anthea strode straight through the cows to the opposite corner of the cow field. When she was directly behind Granny's garden she sat down on the old tree stump that we sometimes use as a pretend car.

We crawled over to Bob and Sally's fence, climbed it and hid in the shaded hazel bushes at the bottom of their garden.

'See,' hissed Tom. 'See!'

Anthea was pointing her binoculars right at Granny's house.

Pip said, 'What if Anthea is planning to do something to hurt Granny and Granny ends up in hospital? What if Granny starts being REALLY POORLY like other people's grannies sometimes are? I don't want our granny to be old and poorly because our granny is still really useful.'

This was probably the most Pip had ever said in one go EVER and I think speaking must have put her in a bad mood because she got so cross that she kicked a stone really hard into Granny's garden. A flock of birds flew up out of the magnolia tree and Anthea looked over towards our hiding place.

'Drat!' she said, crossly. 'I'll have to come back later.'

Anthea stood up and walked towards us. We were well hidden in the hazel bushes, but I had a feeling that Anthea might be able to see THROUGH hazel. I held my breath for so long I was about to stop breathing. I thought, what if Anthea captures us and locks us in a cupboard under the stairs? What if she makes us walk through the cow field ON OUR OWN?

Soon, Anthea was so close to us I could hear the sound of her humming. I grabbed Pip's hand and closed my eyes and I counted to ten really slowly because that is what my teacher tells us to do if we are having hysterics.

But then the footsteps started getting quieter and after a while I couldn't hear Anthea humming any more and when I opened my eyes she was walking away from us, back towards her own garden.

Tom didn't get annoyed with Pip for kicking the stone and nearly blowing our cover because for one thing the stone incident had scared Anthea away. Plus, we could both tell that Pip was REALLY worried about Granny.

'When grannies get old and poorly,' said Pip, swallowing hard, 'they have to go and live in an old people's home and if Granny goes into an old people's home we won't be able to stay with her any more.'

This made us all feel faint and gulpy.

'That's what happened to Davey Pike,' said Tom, nodding. 'Davey Pike's granny used to look after him in the holidays, but she started calling him Daisy instead of Davey. Then she forgot to lock the front door and Davey tried to walk home across a dual carriageway, and now Davey has to go to Little Masters Art Camp every holiday and Davey Pike hates Little Masters way more than he hated his granny calling him Daisy.'

Pip, who was now doing a backbend, said, 'I can't go to art camp. Art camp would scar me for life.' (Another thing about Pip is that she is allergic to doing new things that she hasn't done before, such as holiday camps and tennis lessons.)

'Maybe we should tell Granny about Anthea?' I suggested because in life I usually feel better if I spill the beans.

But Tom shook his head. He said that WE were the ones who had DISCOVERED this worrying situation so WE had to take responsibility for it. Tom is really keen on TAKING RESPONSIBILITY. His dad (Uncle Marcus) says children should think for themselves. That's why Tom and Pip don't get any help with homework and they're allowed to make cups of tea with the boiling hot kettle and they can walk to school on their own too.

Uncle Marcus says that compared to Tom and Pip I am a pampered little prince, but I don't mind being a pampered little prince because I can't do my homework without help and if I walked to school on my own I wouldn't have anyone to chat to. Also, I'm not very good at coming up with sensible ideas.

But luckily Tom IS. He told me and Pip that he didn't think Anthea was trying to HURT Granny, she was just trying to get her hands on Granny's recipe – that's why she was pointing her binoculars right at Granny's kitchen. Tom also said he was going to start writing down EVERYTHING like a proper investigation so we could produce hard and fast evidence at the drop of a hat.

And this was such an AMAZING idea that straight away me and Pip felt a bit less worried and we also felt really hungry.

So we wandered up the garden to see what was for lunch.

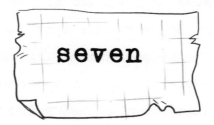

seven

Granny was in a really good mood because baking Layer Number One that morning had gone really well.

She said 'Goodo' and 'Hmmmm' a lot and she kept nibbling crumbs of chocolate sponge and smiling.

She was so happy with her morning's baking she forgot to tell us to wash our hands before lunch, but luckily she DID remember that Pip doesn't like ice in her water (if Pip so much as glimpses an ice cube she starts remembering about the iceberg in the film *Titanic* and then she goes even quieter than usual because she can't stop thinking about all the passengers who didn't manage to get into a lifeboat, especially the people in the orchestra who kept playing sad songs on their violins when the ship was sinking).

But even though lunch was pizza (which is our second favourite food after hot dogs and macaroni cheese) we didn't gobble it up at top speed like we usually do because Tom was busy trying to write up his Investigation Notes at the same time as eating, and me and Pip were watching him.

Tom was using the new fountain pen with green ink that he got for his birthday the week before, except the green ink went really smudgy because the only thing he had to write on was a paper napkin.

This is what he wrote:

INVESTIGATION BAKE OFF

True life facts:

Granny is worried that her neighbours will 'get their hands' on her secret recipe.
Granny's neighbours have been discussing Granny's secret recipe in broad daylight.

Possible suspects:

Ronnie Mehta - he told Anthea to keep him posted about spotting 'our elusive friend'.
Bob Merry - he found out about Granny's secret recipe and told the others.
Anthea -

1. She used to be a spy so she definitely knows what she is doing.

2. She said to Ronnie Mehta, 'Once a spy, always a spy'.

3. She used binoculars to spy on Granny.

4. Anthea is not a pleasant person.

Tom chewed his pen and looked at me and Pip.

'Well,' he said, 'the evidence mounts up against Anthea. She's definitely our chief suspect. But what next?'

Me and Pip looked at Tom all blankly because usually Tom is the best person at ideas and it was a bit unusual that he was asking us what to do. I tried really hard to think of an idea but I kept thinking of other things instead, e.g. football and how much pocket money I had left.

But then I forgot to think about anything because at that exact moment I spotted a cat sitting on Granny's patio and then all I could think about was making friends with that cat because the main thing about me is that I am mad about animals.

'Look,' I said, all happy.

Tom and Pip stared at the cat too and for about thirty-two seconds none of us said anything because it was quite a strange cat.

Its fur was black and ginger and white, but you

couldn't really see the white because it was so dirty and the ginger bits were slightly bald. Its feet were a sort of yellowy colour and its ears had funny marks all over them. Also, it had staring eyes that did not blink. It definitely wasn't one of Anthea's cats because it didn't have a collar or a bell.

'So!' said Granny (who hadn't noticed the cat). 'What are you lot going to do this afternoon while I'm baking cake Layer Number Two?'

We looked at each other all wibbly because we couldn't tell Granny what we were REALLY planning on doing that afternoon – i.e. keeping HER EVIL

SPYING NEIGHBOUR away from her recipe, because:

> Granny didn't KNOW that her neighbour WAS an evil spy
>
> She didn't know that her recipe was in danger
>
> We didn't want to start worrying her because you can't be too careful with old people and their rickety hearts.

That's why I had to tell a fib and say something without thinking.

I said, 'Tom is writing a PLAY and we are his researchers and one of the characters in the play is an old woman so we need to keep an eye on you because we are using you as our case study because you are a woman and you are also quite a bit old. And we also need to keep an eye on your neighbours because they are not as young as they used to be.'

I actually thought this was quite a good fib of mine, but Granny opened her eyes very wide. It looked like she was going to get cross but she didn't, probably because I'd told her we were writing a play and one thing I have noticed about grown-ups is that if you say you are writing a play they don't mind anything because writing keeps children quiet for ages and it is educational.

But I DID feel bad for telling Granny that she was old so I patted her on the arm and said, 'We think you are a fine specimen for your age.'

Tom and Pip also smiled really hard to make Granny feel better about being old but Granny snorted.

'Hmmmmm!!' she said. 'Well in that case you'd better start writing that play on the double, before I start to wither and decay and become a GRUMPY specimen instead.'

And even though we knew Granny was sort of

joking, we also knew that she wasn't in the mood for messing around.

'But,' said Granny, 'if you're writing a play, make sure you use scrap paper. No getting fresh stuff from my desk.'

Granny narrowed her eyes when she said this and pointed to a pile of scrap paper on the edge of the kitchen island. Granny's scrap-paper pile is really high and the reason she keeps it in plain sight is so we can never say we can't find it.

One big rule in Granny's house is that you have to use BOTH sides of all the paper in the scrap-paper pile BEFORE you are allowed to use fresh paper. Our granny is not keen on waste. She prefers to save the environment.

That's why after lunch, when Granny settled down with her secret recipe to make Layer Number Two, we grabbed a handful of scrap paper and pretended to write a play, even though what we were REALLY doing was writing more Investigation Notes. Tom wrote:

Plan of Action 1:

Don't let the recipe out of our sight.
Don't let Anthea inside the house.
Make friends with the cat.

I was really pleased to read the bit about making friends with the cat because that was secretly what I'd been hoping to spend the afternoon doing. I didn't know what it had to do with the investigation, but Tom explained that when it comes to tracking down spies you can't leave any stone unturned. And when I asked him what that meant, he tapped his nose and told me not to worry. So I tried not to worry and Pip stood on her head and then the doorbell rang.

Granny said, 'Get the door for me, someone,' and that someone had to be me because Tom was writing his Investigation Notes and Pip was upside down – and all I was doing was licking leftover cake mix out of a bowl which doesn't count as being busy.

But when I opened the door I knew I had to start concentrating. It was a bit like how I feel at school when it's time to hand homework in and I realise that I have left mine at home and will have to stay in at lunch again unless I think on the spot and make up a really good excuse. Except this was more serious even than homework and it was possibly a life-threatening situation because THE PERSON AT THE DOOR WAS ANTHEA.

'Hello, Joseph,' said Anthea, all pretend friendly. 'Is your grandmother in?'

I wondered if she'd gone back into the cow field after we'd left because she was still carrying her binoculars.

'She's busy,' I said in a slightly rude voice. 'She's baking.'

'Is she now,' said Anthea. 'Preparing for the Bake Off, is she? What's she making?'

'I'm not allowed to say,' I said. 'It's top secret.'

Anthea roared with laughter. 'Ha!' she said. 'Good for you, boyo.' Then she lowered her voice and said, 'Go on,

Joseph, let the cat out of the bag. I won't tell anyone.'

I remembered about Anthea admitting she was a spy and then I remembered what Tom had said about how Anthea would do anything to get her hands on Granny's recipe and I remembered Pip asking if Anthea would ever do anything to HURT Granny. And then I remembered about our Plan of Action and what Tom had written down about not letting Anthea get near Granny. So I tried to shut the door in Anthea's face.

At this point my heart went all gallopy because shutting the door in somebody's face is a really rude thing to do. And even though we suspected Anthea of trying to get her hands on Granny's secret recipe, we still didn't have evidence. Also, Anthea is a grown-up and shutting the door in a grown-up's face is REALLY BAD BEHAVIOUR.

I saw what Tom meant about bad things always happening when Anthea is around. But Anthea didn't seem to notice that I was shutting the door in her face.

She just pushed past me and sailed into the kitchen.

'Afternoon, Jenny,' she said, whooshing onto the chair I'd been sitting in and plonking her binoculars on the table. She stared at my bowl of cake mix and then she turned to Granny and said, 'Any chance of a coffee?' and sighed.

One thing I'm not keen on is grown-ups who sigh. Granny never sighs and Mum only does on special occasions, for instance Parents' Evening.

'Well, Jenny,' Anthea said, 'what we all want to know is what you're baking for this year's Great Village Bake Off.'

Granny filled up their coffee cups and smiled. 'That,' she said, picking up her grandmother's recipe and popping it into her apron pocket, 'is top-secret information.'

'Oh indeed?' said Anthea, peering at Granny's apron pocket.

(Except I don't think Granny noticed Anthea peering at her apron pocket because she was emptying two

packets of butter into a mixing bowl.)

'What about you, Anthea?' Granny asked, wiping buttery hands on her apron.

'Not sure yet,' Anthea said, smiling to herself. 'I'm a last-minuter. Need to wait till inspiration strikes.' Anthea paused and narrowed her eyes. 'Go on, Jenny,' she said. 'Spill the beans – what IS this secret recipe of yours? I'm dying to know.'

But Granny didn't bother answering. She ducked into the larder and laughed.

'Never mind,' said Anthea, smiling. 'If you won't tell me, I'll just have to get it some other way.'

And then Granny and Anthea both laughed and started talking about mean Phil in *Cul-de-Sac* because mean Phil is one of their favourite subjects of conversation.

Me, Tom and Pip gave each other a worried look. We HAD to get Anthea out of the kitchen before she got her hands on Granny's recipe. Luckily Tom was a fast thinker.

'Oooh!' he said suddenly. 'What's wrong with that strange cat!'

Anthea stopped talking about mean Phil from *Cul-de-Sac* and stood up straight away because remember she is mad about cats.

'What cat where?' she said.

We led Anthea out onto the patio and stared at the strange cat for a long time.

'The poor mite,' said Anthea. 'He looks half starved.'

Anthea took some homemade cat snacks out of her pocket and placed them on the patio. Then she gave the cat a quick stroke on its neck and peered into its eyes with a funny expression on her face. She stayed like that for a really long time and then, for the first time since we'd seen it, the cat started to purr.

Straight away me, Tom and Pip were really shocked because that cat's purr was not normal.

'Does that sound freaky to you?' said Tom and I nodded because it did.

'Are they calling you freaky?' said Anthea in the

baby voice she always uses when she talks to cats. 'Are they being VERY rude?'

Tom told Anthea that, actually, he and Pip knew quite a lot about cats because they have two cats of their own at home in Wales. He said he knew for a fact that this was not a normal purring sound, but Anthea just smiled.

'Well, folks,' she said, giving the cat one last stroke. 'If I were you, I'd stay away from this particular cat.'

We smiled at Anthea because Tom is always telling us that it helps to keep your enemy onside until you have hard and fast proof – and also because smiling at grown-ups and looking at them in the eye is called being polite. But as soon as Anthea had gone we stopped smiling and headed upstairs to our bedroom.

Tom said you can tell a lot about a suspect from their throwaway remarks and he started writing down all the suspicious throwaway remarks that Anthea had made. Except when he wrote them down in a list they did not make much sense.

Anthea's suspicious throwaway remarks:

'If you won't tell me, I'll have to get it some other way.'
'Let the cat out of the bag'
'Are they calling you freaky?'
'Stay away from this particular cat.'

'I wonder why she wants us to stay away from that particular cat?' asked Tom, chewing his lip.

I leaned out of the window. 'It's STILL there,' I said. 'It's STILL STARING at Granny.'

'Is it?' said Tom, scratching his chin. 'IS IT?'

'Look what I've got,' said Pip and pulled out something from under her jumper, and when I saw what the something was I had to concentrate REALLY hard on not shouting at the top of my voice and giving the game away because the thing that Pip was hiding under her jumper was . . . Anthea's binoculars.

eight

Me and Pip were really happy because we thought that, now we had stolen her binoculars, Anthea wouldn't be able to spy on Granny any more and we could go back to playing football and eating ice lollies. But Tom was still worried.

'We can't afford to get complacent,' he said. 'Remember we are dealing with a true-life spy. Anthea is too clever to rely on one method of spying so I am guessing she is using a two-pronged attack.'

I wasn't sure what a 'two-pronged attack' meant but it sounded dangerous and it also sounded like it might get in the way of playing football and eating ice lollies.

'We have to assume,' said Tom, 'that Anthea has an accomplice.' He paused and looked at me and Pip. 'I have a good idea where to start looking.'

Tom led the way down the stairs and outside. Straight away I started biting my nails because I did not fancy going back into the cow field again, but luckily Tom stopped when we got to Granny's patio and pointed at the weird cat.

'That,' he said, 'is no ordinary cat.'

My favourite animals are dogs, but if dogs aren't on offer I'll take anything. At home I have a goldfish called Bubble and a stick insect called Ralph and even though Bubble and Ralph are not the most exciting pets on the planet, they are still better than no pets at all.

In Wales, Tom and Pip have loads of exciting pets. They have three dogs and two cats and one guinea pig and an old tortoise called Dave (named after David Attenborough). And also they live next to a farm so they sort of have hundreds of sheep too.

When we grow up, me, Tom and Pip are going to start our own farm and any animal will be welcome, including dangerous ones. We even like spiders. We're not fussy. But Tom was right, there was something really strange about that cat.

'Hello, kitty,' I whispered, stretching out my hand.

The cat turned its head slowly and glanced at me. Except when its head turned, it was all jerky, a bit like a robot. Then it went back to staring through Granny's French doors.

I tried again.

'Here, kitty cat,' I said softly, moving a little closer.

The cat turned again (all jerky) and made a strange hissing noise that sounded more like beeping.

I backed away and Tom scribbled comments down in his Investigation Notes.

'Hello, you lot,' said a friendly voice from over the hedge. 'What are you up to?'

It was Bob Merry. He was standing next to Sally and they were both smiling which was not unusual or suspicious because Bob and Sally are the smiliest people we know. They are even smilier than Dawn, my school lollipop lady, and that is saying something.

I pointed at the cat. 'We're making friends with this cat.'

'Good grief,' Bob said, chuckling, 'I wouldn't want to meet that on a dark night.'

'Bob,' said Sally, beaming. 'You know what they are like. Don't go putting silly ideas in their heads!'

And Bob laughed. After that we chatted to Bob and Sally for a few minutes because they wanted to hear all about my pets, Bubble and Ralph, and about Tom's cricket team and Pip's gymnastics club and we couldn't just say 'yes' and 'no' because 'yes' and 'no' is not making proper conversation. Except Pip didn't even say 'yes' or 'no', she just nodded and stared and let me do mainly all the talking which was fine by me.

But then, eventually, Bob said he had to go back home to make his Great Village Bake Off cake, which was made of beetroot and cream cheese.

'So tell me, folks,' Bob said, laughing, 'don't you think that sounds like a winning combination?' and we nodded even though a cake made of beetroot sounded really quite horrid.

We waved goodbye to Bob and Sally and turned back to the cat. Straight away it made the strange whirring and beeping sounds again. Tom said, 'Hmmm,' and scribbled more comments in his Investigation Notes.

'What is it?' asked me and Pip.

'I'm not sure yet,' said Tom, 'but something is not right.'

'Maybe the cat is just really shy,' I said, 'and maybe if it gets to know us, we could tame it and turn it into our pet.'

I thought this was quite a good suggestion because if we managed to tame the cat really well, Mum might let me take it back home to London (because even though Bubble and Ralph are better than no pets at all, they are still not as good as a real-life cat).

But even though I tried REALLY, REALLY HARD to make friends with that cat, every time I went near it, it kept making those same weird whirring and beeping sounds.

I got it a saucer of milk from the kitchen and Pip made it a toy out of her old rabbit teddy and a piece of string, but the cat ignored the milk and the toy and it ignored us too.

All it wanted to do was stare through the window into the kitchen where Granny was still baking. Tom scribbled some more notes and said he needed to go inside to think in peace. So then I suggested that me and Pip should stop TRYING to make friends with the cat and see if that helped the situation because, in my experience, trying your best doesn't always work.

Like, for instance, at school whenever I TRY to work hard and concentrate, my brain goes all wiggly and I can't even remember how to spell simple words like 'was' and 'how'. But if I'm NOT TRYING HARD, I can remember even tricky spellings, for instance 'necessary', off by heart, WITHOUT EVEN THINKING.

Mum says the problem with me is that although I'm not a trier I can be rather trying – and then she gets the hysterics even though it isn't actually funny.

But even when we stopped trying to make friends with the cat and ignored it, it STILL wasn't interested in us. So in the end I dared Pip to get our football out of the cow field (because as well as being quiet and good at gymnastics, Pip is also the bravest when it comes to cows). And then Pip and I played football and got really, really hot and sweaty.

I didn't think about the cat again until that evening when we were getting in Granny's car to pick up a takeaway from the fish and chip shop in the next village. It was sitting by a bush in Granny's front garden and it stared at us until we disappeared round the corner. I wound down the window and listened. It was still making the whirring and beeping sounds.

In the car, Granny told us that Layer Number Two

had turned out really well too. 'Not even Bob will be able to beat me this year,' she said happily. 'My grandmother's recipe is a winner. I quite fancy my chances.'

Tom tried telling Granny that she needed to keep an eye on her grandmother's recipe because it may be in grave danger, but she just walked into the fish and chip shop, laughing loudly and hooting like an owl.

nine

Breakfast at Granny's is better than at home because Granny buys multipacks of cereal and we can eat as many packs as we want (as long as we finish every single scrap). We're also allowed to sprinkle sugar on top which we're never allowed to do at home because our mums and dads think cereal is packed full of sugar even though the adverts on telly say it's good for you.

It was the day before the Great Village Bake Off and I was on my third bowl of Coco Pops when I noticed the cat again.

It was sitting on the patio and it was staring at Granny, who was about to start baking Layer Number Three.

She added sugar to a bowlful of egg whites and started beating them together in her food mixer.

'Nice and fluffy,' she said happily. 'Snowy peaks.'

I turned to Tom and Pip.

'The cat is STILL there,' I hissed.

'I know,' said Tom. 'It hasn't moved. It's been there all night, staring through the window. I got up every hour to check.'

I took a deep breath. 'Do you think it might have been hypnotised?'

Pip dropped her spoon on the floor with a loud clunk.

'Shhhhhh,' Tom said, pointing at Granny.

Luckily, Granny was busy sieving flour.

'You're barking up the wrong tree,' hissed Tom. 'There is no way the cat could have been hypnotised because when our dad was hypnotised to make him stop smoking, he didn't sit still and stare, he became REALLY BUSY. Like for instance, when the hypnotist told him to jump up and down like a frog, he just did it without complaining. And afterwards he said he couldn't remember being hypnotised or being told to jump up and down like a frog – and he also couldn't remember about not smoking. And now he doesn't trust hypnotists as far as he can throw them.'

Tom paused.

'But,' I said, 'maybe someone has hypnotised the cat to sit still and stare? What about that sort of hypnotism?'

Tom told me I didn't understand hypnotism **AT ALL** which was a bit annoying but also true. And Pip said that she didn't think the cat had been hypnotised because Uncle Marcus's hypnotist said that even though he could hypnotise **ANYONE, ANYTIME, ANYWHERE**, he had not yet mastered the art of hypnotising animals, apart from the odd cobra.

I said, 'Oh,' and then I thought for a bit and said, 'But if it hasn't been hypnotised, why won't it stop staring at Granny?'

Tom jotted down some more Investigation Notes on a crumpled piece of scrap paper and looked up at us. He cleared his throat. 'I've given this a lot of thought,' he said. 'I was up half the night considering our options and I have come to the conclusion that the cat is spying on Granny. Basically it's a spy cat.'

Me and Pip stared at Tom and then we stared at the cat and even though I knew deep down that there was no such thing as a spy cat, I couldn't help wondering if Tom had a point. But then Tom stopped speaking because the phone rang and when Granny went to answer it, the cat's eyes followed her as she walked across the kitchen.

I could tell that the person phoning was Anthea because Granny said, 'Oh hello, Anthea', which was a bit of a giveaway. Granny also said 'Really?' and 'Gosh,' and 'I'll have a look for them!' And then she said, 'Be quiet you lot,' because me, Tom and Pip were talking in loud voices and Granny said that she couldn't hear herself think, let alone listen to Anthea.

So we stopped talking and tried to eavesdrop on Granny and Anthea's conversation, but then Granny put the phone down and said, 'I don't suppose you lot have seen Anthea's binoculars have you?' and her eyes went all small and glinty.

Tom said, 'What binoculars?' and I nearly choked on

my Coco Pops and Granny said, 'Hmmmmm,' and started looking for Anthea's binoculars behind cushions and under newspapers.

Tom turned to me and Pip and made his voice really, really quiet. 'Remember what Granny said about how Anthea used to invent robots for the government?'

Me and Pip nodded.

'And remember how much Anthea LOVES cats and, also, remember about Anthea being obsessed with Granny's recipe and wanting to win the Great Village Bake Off?'

Tom paused to check we were listening properly. He took another deep breath and said: 'What if Anthea invented this cat to spy on Granny? What if it's a ROBOT SPY CAT?'

I could tell in less than a millisecond that Tom was DEADLY serious. For one thing, Tom is not the sort of person to make things up and for another thing he isn't silly like me and for an extra thing, he is really clever.

In other words, Tom had a point.

'What about evidence and proof?' said Pip, because evidence and proof are two of Tom's favourite things in the world. He is mad about them.

Tom grabbed another piece of paper from Granny's pile of scrap paper on the kitchen island and started writing.

'Firstly, look at its eyes,' he said, scribbling at top speed.

I turned to look at the cat's eyes and the more I looked at it the more I knew what Tom meant.

Its eyes weren't shiny and twinkly like most cats', they were blank and dark – a bit like the lens on Tom's camera that he never lets anyone else use.

'And remember the way it purred?' said Tom. 'It sounded JUST like a broken computer.'

We nodded.

'And listen to that beeping sound it makes,' said Tom, leaning towards the patio. 'It's EXACTLY the same sound a robot makes.'

At this point we went quiet and tried to listen.

But we were so quiet that Granny got suspicious and told us to go and be secretive somewhere else. So we forgot to go upstairs and brush our teeth and went outside instead.

In the garden, we studied the cat more closely.

'Also,' said Pip, tiptoeing towards the cat, 'look at the way it moves its neck.'

The cat looked at us, turning its head jerkily and beeping JUST like a robot. It kept making strange whirring sounds, JUST like a computer, and its eyes were all black and staring, JUST like a camera lens.

Tom stopped scribbling. He now had four pieces of scrap paper covered in his Investigation Notes.

He sat down against the wall and read through them, nodding to himself.

'I think this robot spy cat is recording everything Granny does and sending the information back to Anthea,' he said.

Pip nodded and I took a deep breath and we all stared at the cat for a really long time.

'But how are we going to stop it?' asked Pip.

'There's only one thing we CAN do,' said Tom, holding up his notebook and showing us the last thing he had written.

Plan of Action 2:

Kidnap the cat.

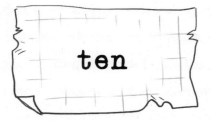

ten

Kidnapping animals has never been a number one priority for me. Mainly because I tend to love all living creatures, including cats.

But this was not an everyday sort of situation and it was not an everyday sort of cat.

Plus, Tom said that in criminal investigations, you sometimes have to do things you don't want to do even if they are tricky and dangerous.

The more time we spent with that cat, the more convinced we became that it was a robot spy cat. It wasn't JUST the black eyes, or the jerky robot movements or the way it purred like a computer, it was also because it was the most vicious cat we had ever met.

Kidnapping that robot spy cat turned out to be very tricky and dangerous – mainly because the cat was keener on biting and scratching than most cats are but also because it kept running away from us. We were now in the front garden, staring at it as it beeped and whirred. My arms were covered in long, red marks and I had a bite on my thumb.

'Anthea must have programmed it to attack humans,' said Tom. 'We're going to need protection.'

Tom disappeared through the front door. When he came out he was carrying a pair of sheepskin mittens, some marigold washing-up gloves and a knitted balaclava. There was an old blanket flung over his shoulder like an enormous scarf.

'Body armour,' he said, throwing the gloves at us. 'Put these on and when I say go, Pip grabs the cat and Joe throws the blanket. Then you'll be able to pick it up and carry it up to our room.'

Me and Pip pulled on the clothes and I got ready to throw.

'Tom,' I said. 'What will you be doing?'

'I'll give the orders,' said Tom. 'Someone has to.'

The robot spy cat wagged its tail

slowly and we all jumped backwards because it is never a good sign when a cat wags its tail.

'Ready?' said Tom.

Me and Pip nodded nervously.

'On the count of three then. Three!'

I tightened my grip on the blanket.

'Two!'

Pip crept forward.

'One!'

Pip put her mittened hands round the cat's tummy and shut her eyes. Her face turned pink and shiny as the robot spy cat hissed and scratched.

'Joe!' shouted Tom. 'Throw the blanket!'

I hesitated for a moment because even though I knew deep down that Tom was probably ninety-nine per cent right about the cat being a robot and not a real animal I couldn't help feeling SLIGHTLY sorry for it.

But then I looked at the scratches on my arms and thought, I'd better do what Tom says because mostly in life he knows what he is talking about. So I took

a deep breath and threw the blanket over the cat. Immediately, it stopped hissing and wriggling and just went very still.

'Why isn't it moving?' said Tom.

'I don't know!'

'Maybe you've killed it,' said Tom.

My tummy went all funny because one thing I try never to do is kill a living creature, not even an ant.

We stood there in Granny's front garden, frozen to the spot.

'What on earth?' said a voice.

It was Sophie Pearce.

She leaned over Granny's front garden fence and stared at us.

Tom took my balaclava and pulled it down over his face and said nothing.

'Erm,' I said. 'We're just helping Granny with her, erm, with some gardening.'

At that moment the robot spy cat started whirring loudly.

Sophie Pearce laughed. 'Yeah,' she said. 'Sounds just like gardening!'

The robot spy cat tried wriggling out of Pip's grip. Any minute it would escape and then we'd have to explain EVERYTHING to Sophie Pearce.

Me and Pip clung on with our fingertips. The cat wriggled again, scratching my arms and trying to bite Pip's finger and the more it wriggled, the more Sophie Pearce stared.

Luckily, just as I was about to drop the spy cat, a ringing sound came from Sophie Pearce's pocket.

She immediately lost interest in us, and picked up her phone. 'Hello!'

'Come on!' I hissed to Pip and we raced into the house.

Tom pulled off his balaclava and stood at the bottom of the stairs while me and Pip carried the robot spy cat up to our bedroom.

That is the funny thing about Tom. He might be REALLY big and strong and clever and he might read loads of books and he might be very good at coming up with ideas but he is not always calm in a crisis.

Like once, when me and Mum were staying at Pip and Tom's house in Wales, me, Tom and Pip were allowed to camp outside on our own without any grown-ups. At midnight there was a massive thunderstorm and Tom FREAKED out and me and Pip had to take him inside to find his mum and he cried his eyes out and refused to go back in the tent. But then the next day, Tom tried to pretend that me and Pip had been scared too, even though we LIKED the sound of the thunderstorm.

Sometimes when Tom falls over and hurts himself Uncle Marcus tells him to pull himself together, but that doesn't help Tom much because it's hard to pull yourself together when you think you are bleeding to death.

One time, I asked my mum about Tom and she said that the world is not black and white and that someone can be brave one minute and frightened the next. She said that most human beings are lots of things at the same time and that is what is so interesting about us as

a species. 'We're all a bit of a mix, Joe,' she said, ruffling my hair. 'Even you can be quiet and sensible from time to time.'

This was quite a good point of my mum's because, for instance, when I am watching a gripping film I stop being a chatterbox and go really quiet. And also I don't tend to be silly at football matches, especially when Kane Ashfield is captain.

But in my opinion my cousin Tom is more of a mix than the average person.

Tom stayed at the bottom of the stairs till the last moment. After ages me and Pip reached our bedroom, shut the door and lifted the blanket off the cat. Then Tom joined us. For a long time the cat stared at me. I stared back at it and bit my nails, but then I remembered that it was a robot spy and its black eyes were cameras recording everything and sending the information back to Anthea so I stopped biting my nails and concentrated really hard on looking NORMAL.

Pip cartwheeled onto her bed.

'Do you think Sophie Pearce will say anything to anyone?'

'No way,' said Tom. 'Sophie Pearce isn't a telltale.'

I did not know how Tom could be so sure about this seeing as he had never actually spoken to Sophie Pearce in his whole entire life, but I did not say anything because when it came to Sophie Pearce, Tom could be a crosspatch.

After that I spent ages trying to make our bedroom comfortable for the robot spy cat because even though it was a ROBOT it still LOOKED like a cat and I couldn't help thinking about its creature comforts.

I grabbed all the pillows and duvets off our beds and put them up in a pile on the floor so it would have a comfy place to sleep. I gave it some of our cuddly toys to play with. Then I fetched it some water from the bathroom (we put the water in the tooth cup because we didn't have anything else) and Tom found some biscuits in his rucksack that he said he didn't mind donating for a good cause. Except the cat didn't even look up when Tom put the biscuits on the floor. Tom said it was probably because robot spy cats don't eat actual food, but I wasn't a hundred per cent sure about this so I went downstairs to get it a bowl of milk from the kitchen JUST IN CASE.

Luckily Granny wasn't in the kitchen because at that moment in time she was chatting to someone on the doorstep. On my way back upstairs, I had a brainwave

and grabbed the hot water bottle from Granny's bedroom and then I filled it with hot water and took it back to our bedroom to keep the robot spy cat really nice and warm and cosy.

After that we spent quite a long time trying to play with the robot spy cat, but it kept trying to scratch us. So in the end we just stared at it and got bored. Eventually we decided it must be lunchtime and we didn't want to make Granny suspicious because we always turn up for lunch. So we gave the robot spy cat a quick stroke, shut our bedroom door tightly and hoped for the best.

eleven

I n the kitchen, Granny was turning everything upside down.

Pans were flying in the air and the floor was covered in flour and icing sugar.

There was no sign of Layer Number Three being made – and no sign of lunch either.

'Bother,' said Granny. 'Bother, bother, bother! Oh hello you lot, how's the play going?'

'Really well,' said Tom because that is mainly what grown-ups want to hear even if it's not true.

'Marvellous,' said Granny, opening a cupboard and rummaging through a pile of Tupperware. 'Oh God, what on EARTH have I done with it?'

My heart went all winky and my mouth turned dry.

'Have you lost something?'

'Hmmm?' said Granny, turning out the contents of her handbag.

'Anything important?' asked Tom.

'Extremely important!' wailed Granny. 'I've lost my grandmother's precious recipe and I need it to make the chocolate fudge icing! I must have put it down in a daft place. I'm such a fool, I could shoot myself.'

Pip gasped and turned white and I think I did too because it was quite a shock to hear that Granny thought the Bake Off was worth shooting herself over. But then I remembered that Granny didn't actually have a single gun in the house except for an old catapult in the attic which only causes tiny bruises.

'Can't you make the fudge icing from memory?' asked Tom.

'Good God no!' said Granny, chuckling. 'I can't remember why I've walked into a room most of the time, let alone memorise a fifty-year-old recipe.'

'When did you last have it?' Tom is good at being

calm and collected if there isn't blood involved.

'Well,' said Granny, accidentally rubbing flour all over her face. 'I had it this morning because I remember putting it in my apron pocket. And a bit later, I got it out and plonked it down on the island so I could make the fudge icing. But then I cleared up the mess you lot made at breakfast and it took ages because I kept finding Coco

Pops in unusual places.' (I twiddled my thumbs because when it comes to spilling Coco Pops, I am the main culprit.) 'And then,' continued Granny, 'Anthea popped over to look for her binoculars,' (Granny gave us a look) 'and after that . . . well that's the funny thing. I can't remember seeing my recipe after Anthea left . . .'

Tom dropped his pen and Pip slightly squawked and I nearly fell off my chair. We could not believe what we were hearing. I was so shocked I thought my ears might burst.

' . . . and the REALLY funny thing,' continued Granny, 'is that I've turned the kitchen upside down and I CAN'T FIND IT ANYWHERE.'

Granny looked at us and shook her head.

'Most odd,' she said.

At that second I felt VERY CROSS. The only time in my whole life that I have felt as cross was the time Dylan Moynihan kicked my brand-new, limited-edition World Cup football over the school fence onto the railway track. But even that didn't make me feel as

FURIOUS as I did right now with Anthea. Anthea must have called on Granny when she knew the coast was clear. When we'd been upstairs guarding the spy cat, Anthea had **STOLEN** Granny's recipe in broad daylight.

But as well as being **EXTREMELY** cross with Anthea, I was also **QUITE** cross with us because if we hadn't left Granny's recipe unguarded for so long while we were upstairs making the robot spy cat comfortable, Anthea would **NEVER** have been able to steal it.

Tom and Pip helped Granny make sandwiches for our lunch, but I sat down on the kitchen floor and did something I don't do very often. I had a good long think.

Normally when there has been a burglary you are meant to call the police, but I was not keen on doing that because a) I wasn't sure if a crumpled old recipe counted as burglary and b) I was quite scared of the police.

'Oh and another thing,' said Granny, wrinkling her nose, 'Anthea was asking about an unusual cat that was in the garden earlier. She wanted to check that it's OK. Don't suppose you lot have seen it?'

'Cat?' I said a bit too loudly. 'What cat?'

'Well if you see it, will you tell Anthea?' Granny said. 'You know what she is like about cats. Oh heavens, I'll just have to fudge this icing – get it, ha, ha, ha! – and see how it goes – recipe or no recipe. I will not be defeated!'

Even though Granny sounded brave I could tell that she was actually feeling REALLY disappointed. She had been so confident that this was her year to the win the Great Village Bake Off.

'But right now,' she said, cheering up, 'it's time for *Cul-de-Sac!*' She looked at us and shooed us out of the kitchen. 'Seeing as it's a sunny day, why don't you take your sandwiches into the garden and leave me to Nasty Phil and his marriage troubles.'

And even though we were A BIT worried about leaving the spy cat in our bedroom unsupervised in case Granny discovered it, and even though we were VERY worried about how Granny was going to make chocolate fudge icing without a recipe, we had to go outside because when it's time for *Cul-de-Sac* Granny won't take 'no' for an answer.

As soon as we got into the garden, we headed over the hedge and fence to Ronnie Mehta's garden. Ronnie Mehta waved at us through the window. We waved back, crept through the branches of the weeping willow tree, and ate our sandwiches.

'I bet Anthea is baking her own chocolate fudge layer cake RIGHT NOW,' Tom said. 'She must know about us kidnapping the robot spy cat so she waited until we were out of the way and then she burgled Granny in broad daylight.'

'I thought I heard the doorbell ring,' said Pip in a muffled voice because she was upside down.

'There's nothing we can do about that now,' said Tom, smoothing out a crumpled piece of scrap paper and hurriedly writing up his notes on the side that didn't have writing on it. 'We need to get that recipe back so that Granny can finish the chocolate fudge layer cake BEFORE Anthea makes one first. But how?'

I told them my idea about reporting Anthea to the police without fail (i.e. straight away) but Tom said we couldn't do this yet because of the police having to cross their Ts and dot their Is. And then he said that even if you have a suspect in mind you can't act on your suspicions until you have three things: motive, opportunity and proof (Tom knows a lot about this sort of thing because he has read more than one hundred and twenty-seven detective books. Tom is cleverer than my whole school put together.)

'We have a motive,' said Tom, 'because Anthea really wants to beat Granny and win the Great Village Bake Off. Right?'

Me and Pip nodded and I tried to make myself remember the word 'motive' because it is exactly the sort of word that impresses people in the playground at school, e.g. Dylan Moynihan and Kane Ashfield.

'And she had the opportunity,' said Tom, 'because we left Granny's recipe unguarded in the kitchen.'

We nodded again and Tom stared at his notes, looking thoughtful.

'But what we don't have,' he said, frowning, 'is proof.' He paused. 'The police are mad about proof.'

Straight away I knew that Tom was right about this because, ages ago when I was six, a robber stole Louis Steadman's skateboard from his car boot when it was parked on our street. And when Louis Steadman's mum told the police about it they asked her if she had proof that the skateboard had actually been in the boot of the car and Louis Steadman's mum had to admit that she didn't have proof and couldn't be a hundred per cent sure and at that point the police said that they had bigger fish to fry, and they also told Louis Steadman's mum that she was lucky her car hadn't been stolen too because her boot lock didn't work properly.

I told Tom and Pip the story about Louis Steadman's skateboard and Tom said that if the police in London hadn't been one bit bothered about a top-of-the-range skateboard being stolen from a car boot, then the Muddlemoor police weren't going to be remotely bothered about a crumpled piece of paper going missing from a granny's kitchen.

Tom said that wasting police time is a criminal offence. He said we couldn't call 999 until we had hard-and-fast proof that Anthea had stolen the recipe – otherwise we could end up in prison ourselves.

I paused and felt a bit hot and bothered because for once in my life I had a good idea and even though it wasn't exactly sensible, it was quite BRAVE.

I thought about my idea for a long time and then I asked Pip for the key to open our secret tin and I emptied its contents out on the mossy ground.

Inside the tin were some old coins, a pack of

fake blood, two boiled sweets that had gone soft and sticky and . . . a stink bomb.

Even though I was quite nervous, I couldn't wipe the smile off my face.

twelve

A few nights earlier, me, Tom and Pip had sneaked downstairs when we were meant to be in bed. Granny was watching telly and we hid behind the sofa and watched nearly a whole episode of *Cul-de-Sac* without her noticing. But then I accidentally gave the game away by shrieking loudly because Phil (who is the main character in *Cul-de-Sac*) said a really bad swear word.

When Granny discovered us watching *Cul-de-Sac*, she sent us straight back to bed but we didn't mind because we had basically seen the whole entire episode by then. And the best bit about the episode (apart from when Phil swore) was when Sheila wanted to go and get her favourite jumper back from Phil's flat, but she had to get Phil out of the way first, so she persuaded the neighbours' children to make a racket in Phil's back garden and when Phil went into the back garden to shout at the children to be quiet and get out of his garden, Sheila sneaked through the front door (because Phil never locks his door) and got her favourite jumper out of the house without Phil seeing. And when Phil found out what she had done, he was LIVID (which explains the swearing).

I reminded Tom and Pip about that episode of *Cul-de-Sac*. I explained that we needed to get Anthea out of her kitchen, just like Sheila had got Phil out of his flat. Then, once Anthea was out of the way, we could let ourselves into Anthea's kitchen and find out where she was hiding Granny's stolen recipe and then we could call the police because we would have hard and fast evidence.

I felt really pleased with myself for coming up with my own plan of action for once.

Tom said, 'Anthea won't fall for children being noisy

in her back garden, she will know it is us.' Pip nodded.

'I know,' I said. 'That's why I've come up with another way of getting Anthea out of the house.'

I took a deep breath and waited until Tom and Pip were both looking at me.

'It's simple,' I said, holding up the stink bomb. 'We gas her out.'

As soon as I said this I started to feel sick because it didn't actually sound simple, it sounded dangerous. But at the same time I knew I had to hold my nerve because Anthea HAD TO BE STOPPED.

Luckily Pip said, 'Wow,' and looked really impressed and Tom agreed that it was a 'GOOD IDEA'.

When Mum says 'Good idea,' it doesn't count because mainly she doesn't mean it. Like, for instance, once I told her I wanted to eat pudding first for a change and she said 'Good idea,' because she was sending a text to somebody at work and not actually listening to me. And when we sat down for dinner and I reminded her about giving me my pudding first, she said 'Don't be silly,' and made me eat a whole plate of fish pie before I had pudding. And fish pie is my second worst dinner after casserole.

But when Tom said 'Good idea,' I could tell he actually meant it because he started to write down a plan of action and when Tom starts to write things down, he means business.

Plan of Action 3.
Stink bomb stake out:

1. Throw stink bomb into Anthea's kitchen
2. Lie low
3. Wait for Anthea to open the French doors
4. Break into Anthea's house
5. Steal back Granny's recipe

Immediately I spotted a problem.

'How are we going to get the stink bomb into the kitchen?' I asked.

Tom grinned. 'I've thought of that,' he said. 'I'll throw it.' And straight away I knew that would work because Tom is really good at cricket.

We climbed over the hedge into Anthea's garden and hid in a large laurel bush. One of Anthea's cats was sprawled in a patch of sun on the patio in front of the kitchen. The French doors were shut, but the high-up kitchen window was open a small crack.

But not even a good cricketer like Tom could aim and throw a stink bomb through a small window like that. If he missed (which he almost definitely would) the stink bomb would fall on to the patio and we would be the ones to get gassed. We only had one stink bomb. We only had one chance.

Inside the kitchen we could see Anthea bustling around.

'I bet she's at it already,' I said crossly. 'I bet she's

making chocolate fudge layer cake right in front of our eyes.'

At this point, I started getting a bit hyper and Tom started writing like a **MANIAC** but Pip did not move a muscle. She stared at the open window.

'I can do it,' she said quietly.

'How?' said Tom, but Pip didn't bother replying because she was busy putting the stink bomb carefully in the pocket of her jeans. Then she started crawling towards Anthea's kitchen window.

We watched and held our breath, praying that Anthea wouldn't spot Pip.

As soon as Pip reached the house she gave us the thumbs up and started to climb up a wobbly wooden trellis that was attached to the wall by the kitchen. The open window was high up and Pip looked very small.

'What if she falls and breaks her neck?' I asked Tom.

And even though Tom said, 'Pip's a really good climber,' I could tell that he was quite worried too.

I crossed my fingers behind my back.

When Pip got to the top of the wooden trellis she gave us another thumbs up. Then she put her hand into the back pocket of her jeans and pulled out the stink bomb. She leaned over, stuck her hand through Anthea's open window and threw it on to the kitchen floor.

I half expected something DRAMATIC to happen, e.g. an alarm or a loud shout, because dropping a stink bomb in Anthea's kitchen was one of the naughtiest things we had EVER done and I could not believe that Anthea wouldn't notice STRAIGHT AWAY.

But there was no alarm and no loud shout. Pip climbed back down the wall and crawled back towards us.

I guessed that maybe the stink bomb hadn't bounced hard enough on the floor because if a stink bomb lands too softly, it won't explode.

Also, I started to worry that maybe my plan had been rubbish.

'YUCK!' came a loud voice from inside Anthea's

kitchen. 'Which one of you lot is responsible for that smell?'

Anthea swung open her French doors and pushed a couple of cats into the garden. 'Good grief!' she said. 'Have you monsters been guzzling the compost heap again? What a pong!'

When Anthea went back inside she left her French doors wide open, just as I'd hoped she would.

I could not believe it. My plan had worked.

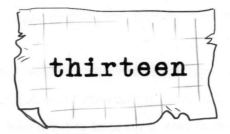

thirteen

We could smell the stink bomb from the garden as we crawled along the grass towards the open French doors.

'It worked,' hissed Tom. 'She's been gassed out of her own kitchen. She's watching *Cul-de-Sac* in the living room. Listen.'

Tom was right. The telly was on in the next room and we could hear Phil and Sheila arguing at top volume.

We tiptoed through the open French doors into Anthea's kitchen. The smell was so bad we had to hold our T-shirts over our noses.

Anthea had DEFINITELY been baking because there were mixing bowls in the sink and a dusting of cocoa powder on the surfaces.

'Let's just find the stolen recipe and get out of here,' whispered Tom, pulling his T-shirt over his nose and scrabbling through a pile of books on the side next to the toaster. 'We need to hurry up before *Cul-de-Sac* finishes.'

The problem was, a piece of scrap paper is not an easy thing to find because in most kitchens there is a lot of paper lying around. We were so busy looking that we forgot to listen out for the *Cul-de-Sac* music and by the time we heard it, it was too late.

'Goodness, it's the Terrible Trio!' said Anthea, striding into her kitchen. 'You're looking very furtive, I must say.'

'Hello!' I said, concentrating on smiling REALLY hard. 'We were just looking for . . .' I paused '. . . something.'

One thing I do a lot in my life is blurt things out when I'm not meant to.

Tom glared at me and I wanted to explain to him that I was just putting Anthea off the scent, but I couldn't actually say anything because Anthea was peering at me with a funny expression on her face.

Then Anthea started to laugh. She laughed so hard that my blood went all fizzy because when a criminal laughs it is NOT a nice sound.

'Biscuit?' said Anthea. 'Cup of tea? Glass of wine?'

I told Anthea that wine was illegal for children, but this made her laugh even more.

'Good for you, kiddo!' she said, and got us all a glass of Coke and some Jaffa Cakes.

We sat down at the table and at that moment escaping from Anthea's house got really tricky because Coke is our favourite drink which we are only allowed on special occasions, e.g. birthdays and at the school summer fair. Plus, it's very hard to say no to Jaffa Cakes.

'You're lucky you weren't here ten minutes ago,' said Anthea. 'One of my cats made such a dreadful smell, I was gassed out of my own kitchen! Had to abandon my baking and watch *Cul-de-Sac* instead!' Anthea roared with laughter.

'Isn't that right, Freckles?' she said, smiling as a large tabby cat slunk back through the open French doors from the garden. 'Not that I EVER mind watching *Cul-de-Sac* of course!'

I was wondering if we should make a run for it when Freckles jumped onto my lap and then I had to stay very still because cats get scared if you make sudden movements. Also, just because Anthea was dangerous and evil, that didn't mean Freckles was.

For some reason, Anthea didn't seem very interested in asking us WHY we were in her kitchen. She was more interested in telling us a story.

The story was all about when Anthea was our age. She told us that she grew up on a farm and she had eight brothers and sisters and she and her brothers and sisters didn't have to go to school and they were allowed to do exactly what they wanted and they were mainly REALLY NAUGHTY.

And then she told us how they used to make traps and spy on the grown-ups a lot and that when she grew up she decided to become a true-life spy for REAL.

The story was really interesting and funny

and I couldn't help listening to Anthea. But then I remembered Anthea's criminal mind and I thought, maybe Anthea is being interesting and funny ON PURPOSE to distract us from thinking she is a recipe thief. Because, after all, Anthea was a true-life spy.

Suddenly I wanted to get out of that house STRAIGHT AWAY. But I couldn't escape because every time I finished my glass of Coke and got ready to leave, Anthea filled it up again.

After a while I started to feel REALLY, REALLY sick and slightly dizzy and sort of like I needed to run around like crazy and that's when I realised something

for the first time: ANTHEA WAS TRYING TO
POISON US.

I put my glass of Coke down and waited until Anthea
turned round to open the fridge. Then I whispered my
suspicions to Pip and Pip spat a mouthful of Coke back
into her glass and nodded.

I told Pip that this was exactly the sort of thing a
dangerous criminal does when they realise someone is
on to them. I said that once on telly an evil spy mixed
some poison into a good spy's cocktail and the poison
made the good spy think the evil spy was a good spy.

I knew that Pip believed me
because she started talking about
escape routes. But when we tried

telling Tom that the Coke was poisoned, Tom did not listen. He said he liked the taste of poisoned Coke and he would not budge from the table. Tom said he wanted to STAY.

At that moment, Anthea walked back towards us with another bottle of Coke. She filled up Tom's glass and she started telling us an easy way to remember the names of capital cities.

I could not believe it.

Anthea was acting as if poisoning children was a perfectly normal afternoon activity.

'Tom,' I said loudly. 'Granny will be worrying about us so we have to go back.'

But Tom was BADLY poisoned. He said 'Yeah,' in a faraway voice. Then he said, 'I'm still a bit thirsty,' and asked Anthea for another glass of Coke.

Making Tom do things he doesn't want to do is quite a hard job for me and Pip. It's normally the other way round. For instance, when Tom wants to sit on Granny's blue velvet armchair to watch telly, he makes me move even though I like the blue velvet chair best too. And on Fridays, when Tom has finished **HIS** sweets, he makes Pip give him some of hers even though Pip likes to make her sweets last all week.

When I told Mum about Tom bossing us around, Mum said that this is what big brothers and sisters and big cousins tend to do and that I am lucky Bella is too busy at university to boss me around. I reminded Mum that when Bella comes home from university she makes me get her glasses of fizzy elderflower and bring her horrible things from the fridge, e.g. olives. And Mum said, 'There you go then!' and gave me a hug.

The thing about Tom is that, even though he is very good at telling other people what to do, it is practically impossible to get him to do one **SINGLE** thing if he doesn't want to do it.

Pip said, 'You'd better do what we say Tom Berryman,' and Tom said, 'You can't make me,' and then they started to get louder and Pip flicked Tom quite hard on the shoulder and Tom said, 'I'll tell Granny on you.'

And it was actually quite embarrassing because Anthea was listening the whole time with an interested expression on her face.

Eventually Anthea interrupted Tom and Pip's argument and told us we were all welcome to stay for as long as we wanted and she said, if it would make us feel better, she could call Granny to EXPLAIN.

But even though Tom was pleased about this, me and Pip were now REALLY WORRIED.

We watched that evil criminal telephone our granny and tell her we were absolutely fine, even though we were actually being poisoned and KEPT AS PRISONERS.

Anthea kept refilling Tom's glass and telling us interesting facts about her job as a spy and about countries we had never even heard of before. And no matter how hard me and Pip tried not to be interested, we could not help it because the poison in that Coke was affecting our brains and making us interested in everything Anthea said.

And the thing is, when a professional spy is poisoning your mind, you can't actually stop them.

We were there for AGES and probably would never have escaped if Granny hadn't telephoned Anthea to say that our dinner was ready. Me and Pip grabbed Tom by the hood of his jumper and we pulled him through the French doors and we ran for our lives.

But Anthea didn't notice that we were running for our lives. She stood in her back door waving and guess what . . .

She was LAUGHING.

fourteen

I t took longer than usual to get back to Granny's because we all felt REALLY sick and Tom had gone all floppy and weird.

Pip said, 'We TOLD you the Coke was poisoned,' in a cross voice and Tom, who isn't scared of Pip's cross voice because he shares a bedroom with her on a daily basis, said, 'I can't help it if I like Coke more than your average person.' Then Tom turned the same colour as the soya milk that my sister Bella keeps in the fridge at home and he sat down in the middle of Ronnie Mehta's garden. Me and Pip explained to him properly about the poisoning situation and eventually Tom believed us and then he was sick all over Ronnie Mehta's geraniums.

But one thing about Tom is that even when he is

feeling sick he is still keen on writing things down so after he was sick we had to wait AGES for him to write up his Investigation Notes on the bundle of paper he had scrunched up in his hoodie pocket.

It took quite a long time because a lot had happened. Tom wrote:

Spying on the Spy

Underneath he wrote all about the stink bomb and the break-in and also the attempted murder (A.K.A. Coke poisoning).

Once Tom had finished writing about Spying on the Spy, he put the stack of notes back in his pocket and we walked across the gardens to Granny's.

'Hello you lot!' said Granny. 'Did you remember to thank Anthea for having you?' and I slightly coughed because even though I normally don't mind the odd bit of fibbing I was beginning to feel that nearly everything I said to Granny was a fib. I was also feeling REALLY bad that we hadn't warned Granny that her friend Anthea was a thief AND a child poisoner. Plus we

HADN'T remembered to thank Anthea.

Granny said, 'I've looked everywhere for that wretched recipe. I've finished the chocolate sponge layers but I'll never be able to make the chocolate fudge icing without it.'

I opened my mouth and thought, Now is the moment to admit the truth and tell Granny EVERYTHING, i.e. about Anthea planting a robot spy cat in Granny's garden to spy on her baking and about Anthea stealing the recipe right from under Granny's eyes. I was even going to tell Granny about Anthea trying to poison us to death.

But just as I was about to speak up, Tom swayed to the left and his eyes went all glittery. Straight away Granny forgot about her missing recipe. She made Tom lie down on the sofa with his legs above his head.

'Has Anthea been giving you Coca Cola?' she asked. (Granny

always calls Coke 'Coca Cola' because she is from a different generation).

Tom said 'A bit,' and I said 'No,' and Granny said 'Hmmmmm,' because obviously somebody was fibbing and that somebody was me. I straight away realised I couldn't exactly tell Granny about Anthea trying to poison us because Granny would never believe a fibber like me.

'Oh and by the way you lot . . .' Granny popped a thermometer under Tom's tongue '. . . there's a funny

smell coming from your bedroom. It is so bad I didn't dare go inside!'

Tom sat bolt upright with the thermometer poking out of his mouth, Pip turned the colour of an old piece of chewing gum and I started biting my nails again. We all knew that the smell was something to do with the robot spy cat because a) it was still in our bedroom and b) we hadn't realised that maybe even robot spy cats need litter trays.

'I'd like you to give that bedroom a jolly good clean and tidy tomorrow,' said Granny, chopping cucumber and plonking it on a plate in the middle of the table. 'That's the only way we can find out what is making that awful smell – I hope you haven't been leaving old sandwiches lying around.'

I slightly giggled because an old sandwich is a long way from a robot spy cat.

Granny looked at me suspiciously as she laid our supper plates. 'Hmmmmm,' she said again, narrowing her eyes.

I went a bit red and also I felt cross with Anthea. If she hadn't been so busy stealing Granny's recipe and trying to poison us we would never have forgotten to check on the robot spy cat and Granny would NEVER have got suspicious. This whole situation was getting more worrying by the minute and it was all ANTHEA'S FAULT.

Granny took the thermometer out of Tom's mouth.

'Completely normal,' she said, 'which is more than I can say about you lot', and then she told us to sit down and eat our sausages. But we couldn't because when you've been poisoned you don't feel hungry at all – not even for sausages.

'Have you been guzzling biscuits at Anthea's too?' asked Granny and I said 'No,' and Tom said 'Maybe,' and Granny said 'Honestly!' and rolled her eyes.

Luckily Granny isn't the sort of person who makes you eat sausages and baked beans when you've been poisoned and even more luckily she's the sort of person who lets you eat apples in front of the telly as long as you promise not to leave the cores lying around on the sofa.

But that evening we couldn't watch telly and we couldn't eat apples either because we HAD TO DEAL WITH THE ROBOT SPY CAT. So we told Granny we felt too tired to watch telly and even though she snorted with laughter when we said this, she said far be it from her to stop us going to bed early.

fifteen

G ranny was right. Our bedroom smelled really bad and straight away I spotted a large cat poo on the floor by the window. Tom was feeling too poisoned to clear up cat poo, so me and Pip held our noses and picked it up using an old plastic bag and then we sneaked out into the garden, treading really softly so Granny wouldn't hear us.

We emptied the cat poo into the compost heap and then Pip suggested filling an old plant pot with fresh soil to use as a litter tray. So we did this and carried it back upstairs.

Luckily the robot spy cat had stopped scratching the carpet and was curled up on an old blanket, whirring and beeping and staring at Tom with its weird black camera eyes.

Tom had his duvet over his head.

'That thing is giving me the creeps,' he said.

'It's not a THING,' I said, but I knew what Tom meant.

I put down the cat litter and we picked up our duvets from the pile we'd left in the middle of the room. Finally, we climbed into our beds. It was really hard to go to sleep, partly because it was still light outside and partly because of the whirring and beeping noises coming from the robot spy cat and also slightly because when you've drunk a lot of poisoned Coke you feel quite full of beans.

I couldn't help thinking that this criminal investigation was getting out of hand. I also couldn't help wishing that we could go back to playing football and making Lego and watching telly and eating apples on the sofa, but I didn't say anything to the others because I didn't want them to think I was scared.

For a long time, we lay in the dark chatting. I told

Tom and Pip about this girl on my street called Casey Hastings who got badly poisoned when she ate her sister's new lipstick set which was from the Pound Shop and full of toxic substances. Casey Hastings had to have her stomach pumped at the hospital because she was allergic to toxic substances. When I asked Casey Hastings why she had eaten the lipstick in the first place, she told me that the lipstick was raspberry bubble-gum flavour and that's why she couldn't resist it.

Tom and Pip were quite interested in Casey Hastings, so I started telling them another story about when she accidentally got locked in the playground after dark, but they fell asleep before I could get to the bit about Casey being rescued by the park warden.

I must have fallen asleep myself because the next thing I knew it was pitch dark and my lighting-up alarm clock said 02:17 a.m. which is the middle of the night. The robot spy cat was fast asleep on the old blanket, but I couldn't get back to sleep because my whole body was itching REALLY badly and when I looked down I noticed that my arms were covered in small, red spots. I lay awake for the rest of the night, trying to ignore the spy cat's whirring snores and trying not to itch my spots and trying not to think about the fact that I might be suffering from a rare and deadly illness.

At 07:03 a.m. I coughed and rustled the pages of

my football magazine really loudly (because one rule at Granny's is that we are not allowed to deliberately wake anybody up). Luckily Tom and Pip woke up and straight away I noticed that their arms were covered in bright red spots too.

As soon as Tom saw the spots he started to panic. He said, 'Get them off me!' and 'Rashes can be deadly,' and

then he said, 'I don't want to die!' and started CRYING.

Pip did not cry because she NEVER cries, but I could tell she was worried because she didn't do press-ups like she normally does first thing in the morning, she just sat in her bed, not moving.

I knew it couldn't be chicken pox because we had all had that one Christmas in Wales and the thing about chicken pox is that you can't catch it more than once. I also knew it wasn't an allergic reaction because when Poppy Symonds eats something she is allergic to, e.g. Mina Kasim's coconut birthday cake, she goes swollen and blotchy, not spotty.

That's when I had a worrying thought. I turned to the others and said, 'What if our spots have something to do with us being poisoned by Anthea?'

Straight away, Tom started screaming hysterically at the top of his voice and the robot spy cat leaped up on to the windowsill, beeping loudly.

'Be quiet!' I said in my firm and sensible voice (which I don't use on a daily basis). 'You're scaring the spy cat. If you carry on like that, Granny will hear you and then she will find out about us kidnapping the spy cat and stealing the binoculars and we will be in MASSIVE TROUBLE.'

So Tom stopped screaming hysterically and started whimpering instead and then he said, 'Why do bad things always happen to me?'

Pip looked up, all calm and collected, and said, 'Is this a life-threatening situation?' And I said, 'I think it might be,' because that was the whole entire truth. And Tom just sobbed. We looked at each other, itching our spots.

'I can hear Granny downstairs,' I said. 'I think we should go and tell her everything straight away. She'll know what to do.'

Tom stopped sobbing. 'No!' he gasped, wiping his nose on his pyjama top. 'We can't tell Granny, Anthea is her friend, she'll never believe us. We'll only get in BIG trouble and be sent home to our parents.'

'But if we've been fed deadly poison,' I said, 'we might die.'

And then Tom started getting hysterics again and Pip chewed her lip.

'This is an emergency,' said Pip, 'and in an emergency you have to call 999 because once a policewoman came into our school and she did an assembly about calling 999 and she said if you call 999 someone will **ALWAYS** be able to help.'

'Are you sure?' I said because one thing I have never done in my whole life is call 999. Calling 999 is **REALLY SERIOUS** and out of bounds.

Pip nodded and Tom sniffed and then they both looked at me.

'But what about proof?' I asked, all gulpy, because I couldn't help remembering that Tom was mad about proof.

Tom took a deep breath. 'I can show them my Investigation Notes,' he said, 'and we can show them our spots and the robot spy cat and

Anthea's binoculars and I bet Anthea has Granny's old recipe hidden away somewhere in her kitchen. That is quite a lot of proof.'

This was true so I nodded but then straight away I wished I hadn't nodded because Tom said he was still a bit too poisoned to make the phone call himself and Pip pointed out that she wasn't the most talkative person on the planet. And then they both looked at me and Tom said, 'You don't mind chatting to grown-ups even when they are far away on the other end of the phone.'

And I could not argue with him because it was the plain and simple truth. But even though I tried to look confident it was quite hard because a) the police aren't like most grown-ups and b) there were butterflies going bananas in my stomach.

sixteen

alling 999 is easy if you know how. The tiny problem was I didn't know how because I had never done it before. And the even bigger problem was that the only phone in Granny's house was in the kitchen and Granny was **IN THE KITCHEN**.

Tom was still panicking about dying from poisoning so Pip picked up his Investigation Notes and grabbed a pen. She wrote:

OPERATION 999

Get Granny out of
her kitchen.
Call the police.
Spill the beans.

The spy cat started making strange noises.

'I think it's hungry,' I said (because one thing I am good at is spotting when living creatures are starving to death).

So Pip put **FEED THE CAT** at the top of the list.

OPERATION 999
Feed the cat.
Get Granny out of
her kitchen.
Call the police.
Spill the beans.

Pip told Tom he had better stop crying and get dressed or she'd tell everyone at school that he was a cry baby and this made Tom stop crying straight away because he never has hysterics in front of people at school if he can help it.

We put on long-sleeved tops over our pyjamas to cover up the spots, but we didn't bother getting dressed because there was no time to lose.

'No scratching,' Tom reminded us as we headed downstairs (because scratching would give the game away).

It was the morning of the Great Village Bake Off but Granny was STILL looking for her recipe.

'I searched for it ALL evening,' she told us, sipping her coffee. 'I'll just have to make bog-standard butter icing. I won't win but at least I'll have a finished cake.'

Tom tried telling Granny NOT to make bog-standard butter icing YET because there was still time to find the recipe and SORT OUT THIS MESS. He kicked me on the shin to remind me about getting Granny out of the kitchen so I could use the telephone to call the police, but I kicked him back and whispered to him about having to feed the spy cat first so we wouldn't have a dead animal on our hands.

Granny stared at us and said, 'What are you bickering about NOW?' and we couldn't think of anything to say so we just ate our breakfast. Even though I am normally quite chatty in the mornings, I barely said one word because I was QUITE worried that the spy cat might die of starvation if I didn't get back upstairs on the double and I was REALLY worried about phoning the police.

I was ALSO a tiny bit concerned about Anthea.

Even though we had proof that Anthea was a dangerous criminal I still didn't love the idea of her being arrested because for one thing, who would look after her seven cats? And for another thing prison cells smell of horrible things, e.g. human wee (my sister Bella told me that last summer when she did work experience at a real-life prison). Plus, Anthea is not as young as she used to be.

'I expect Bob or Anthea will win the Great Village Bake Off again,' said Granny. 'One of them usually does. Any idea what Anthea was baking when you were round there yesterday?'

Pip took a deep breath and Tom pretended to be writing and I just hummed because humming is a useful thing to do if you don't feel like answering.

'Hmmmmm,' said Granny, peering closely at my cheeks. 'You look a bit spotty. I hope you're eating enough vegetables.' And I smiled and told her I was even though I hate most vegetables except sugar snap peas.

After breakfast, I dashed upstairs and left some Coco Pops for the spy cat in a pile on our bedroom floor. The spy cat gobbled them up straight away and stared at me.

'We're not cross with YOU,' I told him. 'It's not YOUR fault you were invented by an evil and dangerous spy.'

But the spy cat just beeped at me so I shut the

bedroom door and went back downstairs.

In the kitchen, Tom was trying to get Granny out of the kitchen. 'It's a lovely day,' he said. 'Don't you want some fresh air?'

Then, when Granny didn't reply, he said, 'Oh look, Granny, your bird feeder needs filling up.'

But that didn't work either because Granny was too busy trying to finish her cake.

'Out of my way!' she said, nudging Tom and smiling. 'I'll come out into the garden with you later but right now I have to FINISH THIS CAKE.' Granny turned on the radio and unwrapped another packet of butter.

'We could try gassing her out like Anthea,' whispered Tom.

'No stink bombs left.'

'What about telling her there's a rat in the bin? She hates rats.'

But this didn't work either mainly because Granny didn't believe us.

We went outside to think of another way of getting her out of the kitchen.

Tom said, 'This is actually Dad's fault for not letting me have a mobile phone till I'm in secondary school.'

I nodded because I knew that Tom wanted a mobile phone nearly as much as I wanted a dog.

'If I had a mobile phone of my own we could have called the police from our bedroom,' he went on. 'It's tragic really. We're all going to die a needless death and a dangerous criminal is going to walk free just because my parents don't think I'm old enough for a phone.'

'Sophie Pearce has a phone,' said Pip.

'I know **THAT**,' said Tom, 'but Sophie Pearce is in secondary school. Anyway,' he continued, 'why are you so interested in Sophie Pearce's pho . . .'

Tom stopped talking.

'Oh,' he said.

Pip did a backflip and grinned. 'We're never going to get Granny out of the kitchen now she's making butter icing,' she said. 'But we **COULD** go over to Sophie

Pearce's house and ask if we can borrow **HER** phone.'

Tom thought for a long time.

'All right,' he said grumpily. 'But for your information, speaking to Sophie Pearce is **A LOT HARDER THAN IT LOOKS**.'

seventeen

The walk to Church Lane took longer than usual, mainly because Tom kept stopping to tie his shoelace and straighten his long-sleeved T-shirt.

'Maybe we should just tell Granny,' he said.

'No,' I said. 'You were right, she would never believe us, not after all the lies we've told her over the past few days.'

'I agree,' said Pip. 'If we want to get Anthea arrested before she wins the Bake Off with Granny's secret recipe, Sophie Pearce is our only chance.'

We walked past the village hall. The car park was full of cars, and people were going in and out with plates of sandwiches and cake stands and jugs of orange squash.

'They're getting ready for the Bake Off,' said Tom. 'We're running out of time.'

'Hi, kids,' called out Ronnie Mehta, who was stringing up colourful bunting with one of his teenage daughters. 'See you this afternoon!'

We waved and I tried to smile but it is hard to look cheerful when you suspect you might be dead by the afternoon.

We walked past the shop and the school and up towards the church. Eventually we got to Sophie Pearce's house. Tom fiddled with his hair.

'I forgot to brush my teeth,' he said.

'Come on,' said Pip. 'Our lives depend on Sophie Pearce's phone and so does Granny's cake.'

Tom shrugged his shoulders because deep down he knew that Pip was right. He took a deep breath and knocked on the door. We heard voices inside and then the door opened, except it wasn't Sophie Pearce, it was her dad and he was really tall and he had a bushy beard.

'Erm,' said Tom in a much deeper voice than normal.

'Is Sophie home?'

'Sure is!' said Sophie's dad, leading us to the kitchen.

Sophie was at the table, texting. She looked surprised to see us.

'Er, hi?' she said.

We stood in silence.

'I'll leave you to it, then!' said Sophie's dad, chuckling

and heading into the garden. Sophie drummed her fingers on the table.

'Ask her,' whispered Pip.

'Shut up,' muttered Tom.

Sophie's phone beeped and she glanced down to read a message.

Tom kept opening his mouth and then closing it again.

'Well, it's been great chatting,' said Sophie, rolling her eyes. 'But I have to go. Chicken crisis.'

Sophie Pearce called goodbye to her dad and headed out.

We followed her on to the street.

Pip kicked Tom really hard. 'Ask her!' she said.

'All right!' said Tom.

Tom turned to look at Sophie Pearce.

'Erm,' he said, in an even deeper voice. 'I was just wondering if my cousin Joe could borrow your phone to make a quick phone call? It's a serious emergency.'

Sophie stared at Tom and burst out laughing. She handed her phone to me at once.

'Sure,' she said. 'No problem!'

eighteen

At first I thought about **PRETENDING** to call the police in order to keep Tom and Pip happy, but then I looked down at the spots on my arms and remembered this was a life-or-death situation. I took a deep breath and dialled 999.

A man's voice on the other end of the phone said, 'What's the nature of your call?' and I gave him a really quick version of the story, even if that's the opposite of what my teacher Mrs Miller tells me to do.

I told him about Anthea being a spy and about the binoculars and the spy cat and the burglary and the poisoning, and I gave him Granny's address and then I said, 'It's a matter of life and death,' and pressed End Call.

I breathed out and felt a bit taller than usual. I thought, when I get back to school I'm going to tell Dylan Moynihan about this and if he says I am being silly and lying I'll tell him he can call the police to check and then he'll know I'm not being silly or lying. I thought, I bet no one else in my class has reported a true-life crime over the summer, not even Florence Harold who goes on holiday to Japan.

I walked over to the others and I gave the phone back to Sophie Pearce and then I gave Tom and Pip a quiet nod and a wink, except I can only actually wink if I hold a hand over one eye.

Sophie Pearce said, 'What's wrong with your eye?' so I took my hand away and tried to wink normally but then I nearly slipped over the curb because when I try to wink normally, I blink and blinking stops you seeing.

By the time I had grabbed on to Pip to save my life, Sophie Pearce was waving goodbye and wandering off in the opposite direction.

'Come on!' shouted Tom. 'We don't want the police arriving at Granny's before we get there.'

We set off back through the village at top speed. The problem was, Granny's house was a mile away from Sophie Pearce's and long-distance running is not my strong point in life. When we were halfway back to Granny's I got a life-threatening stitch and had to stop.

Suddenly I spotted the entrance to The Gravels and stared at the shaded footpath, lined with hedgerows and wildflowers. It didn't seem THAT scary.

'Shall we take the shortcut?'

'No!' said Tom. 'The Gravels is haunted, remember.'

But for the first time in my life I decided to ignore Tom. For one thing, The Gravels didn't even LOOK haunted and for another thing my whole stomach felt like it was on fire. Braving The Gravels suddenly seemed a lot easier than having to run the whole long way back to Granny's with a life-threatening stitch.

'I don't believe in ghosts,' I lied. 'I'm taking the shortcut,' and I set off down The Gravels without looking back.

After a minute or two, I checked behind me, hoping to see Tom and Pip, but there was no sign of them. They had taken the long route. In other words, I was completely on my own.

It was quiet in The Gravels, and cold because the bushes on either side of the path had grown over to create a ceiling of leaves and twigs. No sun could get through.

A twig snapped and I shivered. I started to run, slowly at first, because I still had a really painful stitch in my stomach. But then I heard footsteps behind me and I started to run a bit faster.

The footsteps got closer. I sped up again. I heard breathing, heavy breathing, and my mouth went dry.

'Help me!' I whispered, not even sure who I was talking to. 'Help!'

The footsteps were right behind me now and I felt a warm breath on my neck. Something touched my shoulder. I knew it was a ghost.

'Go away!' I screamed. 'Leave me alone!'

I tripped over a root and fell face first on the grassy path. I lay there panting, not daring to look round.

The ghost started to speak, except it didn't sound like a ghost. It sounded like someone I knew. I opened my eyes and turned around. Tom and Pip stared down at me.

'You didn't think we were going to let you brave The Gravels on your own, did you?' said Tom, helping me to my feet.

It felt like the best moment of my life, even better than the time I scored a last-minute goal against Kane Ashfield.

'Come on,' said Pip, taking my hand. 'Let's get out of here before the real ghosts come.'

We ran on through The Gravels, shouting at ghosts each time we approached a blind bend and, finally, **FINALLY**, we saw a chink of light.

'There's the stile!' shouted Tom. 'We're nearly there.'

I knew that beyond the stile was daylight and the main road. We sped up, leaping over roots and brambles. At last we leaped over the stile and burst onto the main road. The bright sunshine made everything feel warm and safe.

'That ghost had better get in training if it wants to

keep up with us next time,' said Tom. And we all started to laugh hysterically. But when we crossed the road and turned into Little Draycott we stopped laughing. Because, parked right outside Granny's house was a real-live police car.

nineteen

The front door wasn't locked so we crept into the hall and listened at Granny's kitchen door. We couldn't hear much, just snippets of conversation, e.g. 'burglary', 'neighbour' and 'at this address'. But then we heard Granny say, 'Good heavens, officers, you'd better sit down!'

At this point, I held my breath for a bit too long because I started to feel wobbly and then I saw little whizzing dots in front of my eyes. I closed my eyes and leaned against the kitchen door, but it wasn't shut properly so it flew open and I landed flat on the kitchen floor. When I looked up, Granny was standing over me with her hands on her hips.

'Here they are, officers,' she said, turning to a man

and woman in police uniforms who were having tea at the kitchen table.. 'My grandchildren. A.K.A. the Terrible Trio!'

The police officers did not smile.

'We believe you may have reported some crimes,' said the woman.

I did not say one word. I did not even grin. For some reason I had slightly lost my voice.

'Quite serious crimes from the sound of things,' she continued. 'And we gather the suspect lives on this road?'

Granny glared at us and so did the police officers and when people glare at me for long enough, I can't help spilling the beans.

I ignored Tom's kicks and told Granny and the police officers that I was the one who called the police. Then I told them about Anthea using binoculars to look at Granny's recipe from the cow field, and how she had invented a robot spy cat to spy on Granny while she was baking, and I also told them about Anthea stealing the recipe from under Granny's nose, and finally I told them about the most serious crime, i.e. about Anthea poisoning us with Coke and giving us a terrible rash. Then I held up my sleeves and pyjama top and showed them the bad rash and luckily it looked REALLY SERIOUS and QUITE DEADLY.

Granny and the police officers examined our

tummies and our arms and legs and they looked at each other.

'Where did you say this Anthea person lives?' said the policewoman.

'Number Five, three doors down,' said Granny, wearily. 'She's a good friend of mine. She used to work for the British government. She's the most law-abiding person I know.'

Granny led the police officers over to Anthea's house and we followed, itching the whole way. It reminded me a bit of the time I accidentally flooded the school toilets and was sent to Mr Rogers's office to discuss my options. Except this was even more scary because at least when I accidentally flooded the school toilets there weren't any police officers involved.

The policewoman knocked on Anthea's door. I expected Anthea to make a run for it when she saw the police but she didn't, she looked REALLY PLEASED.

'Come in, come in!' she said, pushing cats out of the way and welcoming everybody into her kitchen.

I looked around to see if Anthea had left a chocolate fudge layer cake lying around in plain sight, but her kitchen was really clean and tidy and there was no sign of a cake anywhere.

'She's been getting rid of evidence,' Tom whispered.

'Well,' said the policewoman, 'it's a bit awkward, but we've had a report of some crimes involving this address and we need to follow it up.'

'Oooh!' said Anthea. 'Yes, I expect you've got to cross your Ts and dot your Is – especially in this day and age.'

Tom gave me and Pip a told-you-so look.

The police officer looked down at her notebook and repeated everything I had told her. The whole time she was talking, Anthea kept glancing at Granny with twitchy lips and eventually Granny started snorting through her nose and then she got a coughing fit and had to borrow a hankie from Anthea to wipe her eyes.

When the police officer finally stopped talking, Anthea thanked her and said she had a few questions to ask us before she was arrested and put in prison for the rest of her life.

Anthea winked and turned to us.

'Excellent detective work,' she said. 'But what I REALLY want to know is, have you done your homework?'

We did not say anything, partly because we try not to do holiday homework until the last minute and partly because we did not know what Anthea was talking about.

'What I mean,' boomed Anthea, 'is did you do the job properly? Did you take notes? Do you have evidence to back up your accusations?'

Tom stepped forward. 'Actually we did,' he said. 'I wrote notes. Look.'

Tom flung his pile of Investigation Notes at Anthea and the two police officers.

'Hmmmm,' said Anthea. 'Well done. I'll just have a quick gander, shall I?'

Anthea flicked through the pile of notes, smiling THE WHOLE TIME.

'Excellent detail – and planning,' she said, studying our Plans of Action. 'And full marks for recycling. Glad to see you're using both sides of the paper.'

'It's one of Granny's rules,' I gabbled. 'She keeps a pile of scrap paper on the kitchen table. We have to use both sides before we get the new stuff.'

'Couldn't agree more!' laughed Anthea. 'But it does rather explain the mix up.'

Anthea held up the most crumpled piece of scrap paper and showed it to the police officers. I leaned over to see what she was pointing at and my mouth turned dry. It felt even drier than the time my friend Theo came over to my flat after school and told me human beings couldn't eat more than one cracker in one go without drinking water so I ate two crackers without taking a single sip and ALMOST DIED.

On one side of the crumpled piece of paper was Tom's Investigation Notes and on the other was . . .

Granny's missing recipe.

Me, Tom and Pip waited for each other to say something, but none of us could think of one single thing that would change the fact that we had mistaken Granny's recipe for an old piece of scrap paper.

WE WERE THE TRUE-LIFE RECIPE THIEVES.

Tom swallowed, Pip sucked her cheeks in, and I

looked down at my shoes which were actually my slippers because I hadn't got dressed properly. When I looked up, all four grown-ups were staring at us.

Tom took a deep breath and started to speak and for a moment I had a last glimmer of hope because Tom is in the debating club at his school and he is used to arguing his point because his dad (Uncle Marcus) is a lawyer and isn't keen on small talk.

'But why were you spying on our granny with binoculars?' said Tom.

'I wasn't spying on your GRANDMOTHER!' said Anthea, exploding with laughter. 'I was trying to spot our elusive friend, the Lesser Spotted Woodpecker. Mrs Rooney saw one in Jeffrey's meadow last week and Bob Merry informed me that he saw it twice in your grandmother's magnolia tree on Thursday.'

Anthea paused and turned to the police.

'The Lesser Spotted Woodpecker is a very rare bird,' she explained and the police officers nodded and made a note of it.

Granny, who was still jiggling up and down and wiping tears from her eyes, didn't say anything. Straight away I remembered about Anthea loving birdwatching and I also remembered about birdwatchers using binoculars and I started to get a bit worried that maybe we had got our facts wrong.

'But what about the spy cat?' said Tom. 'And also what about you making us ill and giving us a rash with poisoned Coke?'

Tom pulled up his T-shirt and showed off his tummy which was still covered in spots.

Anthea peered at Tom's tummy.

'Hmmmmmm,' she said, 'it certainly COULD be the result of Coca Cola poisoning . . .'

Tom nodded at me and Pip.

'But then again . . .' Anthea interrupted, 'it also looks remarkably like flea bites. Where exactly did you say you'd hidden this spy cat of yours?'

Tom paused for a moment and swallowed. 'In our bedroom,' he said.

'And did you leave anything out for the spy cat to sleep on?'

Tom's voice went very, very quiet. 'Yes,' he said in barely a whisper. 'Our duvets and blankets.'

Anthea's kitchen started to swirl.

'Bingo!' said Anthea, grinning at the open-mouthed police officers. 'Bob's your uncle! Poisoned Coke, my old pinny. These young detectives are covered in flea bites.'

The room went quiet. Even Tom stopped trying to argue.

'Right,' continued Anthea, 'I think before we do anything else we'd better rescue this poor cat from this bedroom of yours and check it is still alive. Come along officers?'

The police officers nodded obediently and followed Anthea back to Granny's.

'We fed it!' I said, running after them. 'We gave it milk and Coco Pops and old biscuits. We even made it a litter tray because even robot spy cats need litter trays.'

But the grown-ups didn't hear me. They were too

busy racing up Little Draycott towards Granny's house.

Anthea flung open our bedroom door. Straight away the robot spy cat leaped off the windowsill and landed on my bed.

'Good grief,' said Anthea, picking it up and holding it at arm's length. 'The poor thing is absolutely riddled with fleas. No wonder the Terrible Trio are covered in bites. This isn't a spy cat, this is a stray and it needs rescuing RIGHT NOW.'

Granny looked at us and shook her head.

'But you poisoned us with Coke,' said Tom quietly. 'I was sick in Ronnie Mehta's geraniums. We might DIE.'

'Nonsense,' said Anthea. 'You drank two litres of Coke. No wonder you were sick!'

The police officers put away their notebooks and picked up Anthea's binoculars which were sitting on top of our chest of drawers.

'I take it these are yours ... Mrs ... er ...'

'Agent three-four-six, at your service,' laughed Anthea, taking the binoculars.

'Thank you . . . erm . . . Agent three-four-six . . . for clearing everything up. Many apologies for wasting your time.'

'Oh not at all!' laughed Anthea. 'This is the most fun I've had since I was in full-time service with MI6. I only wish I COULD invent a robot spy cat. Maybe that could be next year's challenge!'

Granny made us say sorry to the police officers and then she made us say sorry to Anthea and then, when Anthea took the spy cat back to her house to give it a bath and treat it for fleas, Granny made us tidy our room from top to bottom and put all the sheets and duvets and blankets in the wash and she even made us clear up all the Lego on the landing, which shows how cross she was. After that she covered us in Savlon and made us swallow flea tablets which tasted a lot worse than poisoned Coke.

When we had finally finished cleaning our bedroom, we crept downstairs. Granny was serving cups of tea to the police officers and cutting slices of chocolate

sponge from the top layer of the cake she had made for the Great Village Bake Off.

I raced up to Granny and told her that she shouldn't be cutting up her cake because she still had time to enter the Great Village Bake Off that afternoon, but Granny just glared at us even more than she had before.

'I'm afraid,' she said in a growly voice, 'that giving away cake is the kind of sacrifice you have to be prepared to make if you go about wasting police officers' time.'

And I could tell that Granny was PROPERLY cross because she cut huge slices of Layer Number One for the police officers and she didn't offer ANY to us.

Not even a sliver.

twenty

A good thing about our granny is that she is a big
believer in second chances. This is the opposite
of, say, my teacher Mrs Miller who says, 'Especially you,
Joe Robinson' whenever she tells us to settle down.

By lunchtime, the police officers had gone back to
the police station and Granny had stopped being cross.
There was now no time to make chocolate fudge icing
but she let us ice the cake with butter icing and she
even let us lick the bowl.

In the afternoon we set off to the village hall for the
Great Village Bake Off, carrying Granny's chocolate
cake which only had two layers now, instead of three,
and didn't look very neat.

The village hall was full of people we knew so we

wandered around, saying hello. Chris Norris was leaning on his bike by the door, trying to pretend he wasn't smoking. Sophie Pearce was standing with her parents, and the Fletton twins were throwing banana at the vicar. Bob wandered over and showed us his beetroot cake which had cheese frosting and real vegetables on top.

'Let's hope it tastes better than it looks,' said Sally, laughing, and Bob laughed too because he loves Sally even more than he loves baking.

Ronnie Mehta came over with his teenagers.

'I have a confession,' he told us, putting his finger to his lips and pointing to a colourful caterpillar cake in the middle of the table. 'I bought my cake in Sainsbury's. Do you think anyone will notice?'

We shook our heads because we didn't want to hurt Ronnie Mehta's feelings, but we were actually lying because anyone could tell that Ronnie Mehta's caterpillar cake was way too neat to be homemade.

But there was no point worrying about Ronnie

Mehta being a cheat because it was obvious he wasn't going to win. On the table next to his caterpillar cake was an enormous pyramid of cupcakes. Each cupcake was a different flavour and each one was decorated with a picture of a cat.

It was **AMAZING**.

'What do you think?' said Anthea, rushing towards us. 'I've even added one with a picture of Tiddles. Look!'

Right at the top was a cupcake decorated with a picture of a familiar-looking gingery cat.

'Who's Tiddles?' asked Tom.

Anthea roared with laughter.

'Don't tell me you don't recognise Tiddles?!' she said.

I peered at the picture and straight away realised that Tiddles was the robot spy cat, just a bit cleaner.

'The police said I was welcome to adopt him so that's what I'm going to do,' Anthea continued, smiling. 'He's the sweetest little chap.'

I stared at the scratches on my arm and the deep bite mark on Pip's hand. I did not say anything.

A bit later, the vicar, Reverend Story, walked onto the stage, still wiping banana off his jacket.

'Good afternoon,' he said, 'and welcome to this wonderful occasion. As always, the Great Village Bake Off brings out the fiercest competition in our community and by the looks of things, the standard of baking this year is higher than ever.'

Reverend Story pointed to Ronnie Mehta's

Sainsbury's caterpillar cake when he said this and everybody laughed, including Ronnie Mehta. 'This year,' continued the vicar, 'our village is honoured to have someone FAMOUS to announce the winner of the Great Village Bake Off.'

The crowd started to whisper.

'Ladies and Gentleman,' said the vicar, 'please give a big round of applause for Mr John Farraday – or should I say, Nasty Phil from our favourite soap opera, *Cul-de-Sac!*'

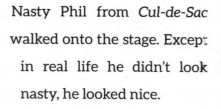

Nasty Phil from *Cul-de-Sac* walked onto the stage. Except in real life he didn't look nasty, he looked nice.

Granny yelped.

'I've known since yesterday,' she said. 'Anthea called round to tell me but it was top secret information so

I've had to keep quiet.'

Granny gazed at Phil from *Cul-de-Sac*.

'The winner of this year's Bake Off gets to have afternoon tea with him,' she whispered. 'It's one of the reasons I was so keen to win!'

The room went silent as Phil/John Farraday started to speak.

'Thank you everybody for welcoming me to the beautiful village of Muddlemoor. I am honoured and delighted to announce the winner of this year's Great Village Bake Off.'

Everybody clapped and cheered.

'I'm told that this year's competition was tougher than ever,' he continued, 'but in the end the judges went for the contestant who showed a range of skills and a special personal touch.'

The room turned quiet and I could hear my heart beating.

Let it be Granny, I thought, digging my nails into the palm of my hand.

'The winner of the 2020 Great Village Bake Off is . . . Anthea Beaumont!'

Everybody cheered as Anthea walked up onto the stage to shake Phil/John Farraday's hand and collect her trophy.

'Good heavens!' said Anthea. 'I'm speechless! Well, almost speechless.' She paused. 'I would like to say a few words.'

The room went quiet.

First Anthea thanked the judges and then she thanked her cats for being her inspiration. Then she made a joke about how she nearly missed this year's competition because of a close run-in with the police and everybody laughed because they thought Anthea was joking, but me, Tom and Pip did not laugh because we were quite busy looking out of the window.

Anthea said how excited she was about sharing afternoon tea with one of her television heroes. Then Phil/John Farraday smiled at Anthea and Anthea went bright red.

'But before you start to party, I would just like to raise your attention to a spot of trouble that has been brought to my attention by Sophie Pearce.'

Anthea pointed at Sophie Pearce, who stopped texting and looked up. Everybody went quiet.

'Sophie informs me that we may have a wild animal hiding out in our village and it has been attacking the neighbourhood chickens. Four were taken yesterday morning and another two were attacked early this afternoon.'

A murmur of chatter broke out amongst the people in the hall.

'It's probably a fox but, looking at the bite marks, we think it might be a smaller creature,' said Anthea. 'So as chair of Muddlemoor Neighourhood Watch, I urge you all to lock up your chickens!'

Anthea smiled around the room.

'But for now,' she continued, 'can everybody PLEASE help themselves to my winning cupcakes. After all, they're not for looking at, they're for EATING!'

Anthea looked exactly like the Queen as she beckoned people towards her prize-winning bake. 'Eat as many as you like,' she said. 'Tuck in!'

The whole village surged towards Anthea's cupcake pyramid and began to help themselves, but me, Tom and Pip stayed at the back of the village hall and watched.

We could not stop thinking about the chickens that had been murdered by a wild animal. We looked at the scratches and bites on our arms and we looked at each other. We knew **EXACTLY** who the chicken murderer was and we didn't like it one tiny bit.

'Not eating my cakes?' said Anthea, wandering over. 'It's not like you lot to turn down sugary snacks!'

Anthea laughed and laughed and laughed.

'Don't worry,' she said. 'I promise I didn't poison them!'

And then she **WINKED** at us very, very slowly.

Me, Pip and Tom went all gaspy. You didn't have to be a genius to realise there was something **REALLY** suspicious about that wink. And you didn't have to be a true-life police officer to know that Anthea and her newly adopted cat were NOT TO BE TRUSTED.

And that's why, even though Anthea's prize-winning cupcakes looked ABSOLUTELY DELICIOUS, we did not take a single bite.

We did not dare.

THE END